THE WESTERN WILDCATS
NOVELLA COLLECTION

JENNIFER SUCEVIC

Always My Girl

Dare You to Love Me

Copyright© 2023 by Jennifer Sucevic

All rights reserved. No part of this book may be reproduced in any form or by any electronic or mechanical means, including information storage and retrieval systems, without written permission from the author, except for the use of brief quotations in a book review.

This is a work of fiction. Names, characters, businesses, palaces, events, locales, and incidents are either the products of the author's imagination or used in a fictitious manner. Any resemblance to actual persons, living or dead, or actual events is purely coincidental.

Cover Design by Claudia Lymari at Tease Designs

Editing by Evelyn Summers at Pinpoint Editing

Proofreading by Autumn Sexton at Wordsmith

Always my Girl

USA Today Bestselling Author
JENNIFER SUCEVIC

1

VIOLA

My cousin links her arm through mine as we trudge across campus for our eight o'clock classes. Our breath forms small clouds in the chilled air as I hoist the travel mug of coffee to my lips. Warmth immediately spreads through my veins, heating me from the inside out. There's not enough caffeine in the world to perk me up this early in the morning. I'm bleary eyed from pulling an all-nighter to work on a paper.

"Remember the Sig Ep party is this Friday and it's Christmas themed. You need to wear an ugly sweater."

"Oh...it is?" The last thing I want to do is spend my night with a bunch of drunken frat guys.

"We're going together, right?"

When I remain silent, attempting to jumpstart my brain in order to come up with a plausible excuse, her voice sharpens.

"Come on, Vi! You promised!"

Shit.

She's right, I did.

Fallyn glares as we weave our way through student traffic.

"Umm—"

That's all I get out before she cuts me off. "Viola!"

I wince as her voice snaps through the chilled air. A few people turn and glance our way.

"I know I promised but…"

We both understand why I'm attempting to bail. It's an issue I've been struggling with since stepping foot on Western's campus this fall.

Her tone turns unexpectedly gentle. "You can't keep hiding out at the apartment."

"Why not?" It's worked so far. Is it really that big a deal if I spend the rest of the academic year holing up there?

She rolls her eyes. "For one, it's not healthy."

I lift my brows. "And two?"

"Vi," she grumbles, irritation bristling in her tone. "Why did you bother transferring schools if you didn't have any intention of actually living your life?"

The question is like a gut punch. It's slowly that I release the air trapped in my lungs as the heavy weight of her words settles on me. "Honestly?"

She nods, waiting for an answer. "Yeah."

"I didn't think it would be this hard." That's an understatement. "It's been three years. I should be over it by now."

Over him.

He shouldn't be anything more than a distant blip in the rearview mirror.

A fond high school memory that ended badly.

My cousin slips her arm around my shoulders and tugs me closer. "Maybe if you put yourself out there every once in a while, you'd meet someone else."

Doubtful.

I never imagined that after three years, he'd still be so fresh in my memories.

"It's not like I haven't tried," I mumble.

The arched brow and steely look in her eyes tells me that she's not buying the load of crap I'm attempting to sell. Fallyn and I have been close since we were kids. The best part of transferring schools has been sharing an apartment with her. It's like having a sleepover every night.

"Not since you've been at Western."

Well…she's got me there.

"No one's caught my eye."

"Probably because you hide out in the apartment 24/7."

"That's not true," I protest. "I go to classes. And the grocery store."

She snorts. "Do you ever converse with the people you come into contact with?"

"Sometimes."

"Liar."

Before I can argue, she says, "Look, I know how much you loved Madden."

The sound of his name is like a dagger piercing my heart. There are times when I wonder if I'll ever be able to hear it without having the same agonizing reaction.

When I remain silent, she pushes onward. "And that he hurt you."

Hurt?

Ha!

More like devastated.

He *devastated* me.

"But it's time for you to move on." She raises an arm and sweeps it toward the campus. "There are a ton of nice guys who attend this school. We need to find one and get you back out there. It's for your own good."

My teeth scrape across my lower lip as everything she said circles through my brain. Deep down, I realize Fallyn's right. But that doesn't make it any easier. Madden and I were together for three years before the breakup. I should have moved on by now, but…

That hasn't happened.

It's not like I haven't tried to get back on the horse again. Several times, in fact. I've had a couple of boyfriends that didn't last long. There was even a drunken one-night stand thrown in for good measure.

But it's not the same.

They're not the same.

"And that starts with the party on Friday night," she says, interrupting my thoughts.

I huff out a reluctant breath. "Fine."

She glances at me with a frown. "Fine? Just like that? You're not going to argue or make me twist your arm?"

My lips tremble with a hint of a smile. First one of the morning.

"Nope. As much as I hate to admit it, you're right. I've spent the past several months hiding, avoiding places I know he'll be, and I don't want to do it any longer. It's exhausting." Not to mention lonely.

She nods approvingly. "Good. I'm glad to hear that."

Just as we're about to swerve toward the Union, a deep chuckle rings out, drawing my attention away from Fallyn. My gaze fastens on the tall, dark-haired guy who looks as if he's holding court. That's all it takes for my heart to clench as my feet grind to a halt.

"Vi?" Her expression morphs into a frown as she follows my line of sight. "Oh."

Yeah. That pretty much sums it up.

Her eyes stay locked on the path that leads to my ex and the fan club vying for his attention as she takes a step in that direction. "Seems like the perfect opportunity to come out of hiding. Screw him. Let the guy see you're here."

That's all it takes for my earlier bravado to vanish.

When she tugs on my hand, I whisper, "You're right about me needing to live my life and not worry about running into Madden around every corner, but...just not right now, okay? I can't deal with it this morning."

I send her a beseeching look and pray she'll take pity on me.

The idea of facing him makes me sick to my stomach. Any moment, my heart is going to explode from my chest.

It was so much easier to avoid him when he came home for the summer or at Christmas. Here at Western, it's been more of a challenge. Even though the campus is sprawling, it's not nearly big enough. I always seem to catch glimpses of him from across a crowded pathway or at the Union. My natural reaction is to duck my head and hope he remains oblivious to my presence. He's either surrounded by teammates or groupies. As much as I don't want to notice the attention he receives from the girls here, that would be impossible. They're constantly fawning over him.

For all I know, he's forgotten about me.

My hand rises to rub the ache that flares to life in my chest.

"All right, fine. I'll let it go this morning, but your time is just about up. Got it?"

I rip my gaze away from Madden long enough to glance at my cousin, surprised by the gentling of her tone. She gives me a slight smile as her eyes flicker to the group of guys for a second time. Emotion creeps into them. It's a potent concoction of sorrow and longing.

I clear my throat. "Fallyn?"

Now, it's her turn to rip her attention away from the hockey players jostling one another.

"Yeah?"

I glance at the guys again, only to find one of them staring directly at her. A little shiver dances down my spine at the possessive look in his eyes.

Maybe I haven't been here long, but I recognize him.

Wolf Westerville.

And I know all about the history between his and Fallyn's family. It's enough to take my mind off my ex.

"We should probably get moving," I say, not wanting to be late for class.

With a nod, her expression smooths out as if she'd never caught a glimpse of Wolf. "You're right. Let's go."

2

MADDEN

Someone needs to tell me what the fuck I'm doing at this frat party.

All I can say is that it was a bad decision on my part.

I lift the bottle of beer to my lips for a long swig before surveying the drunken crowd. The beat of the music reverberates off the walls as people grind against each other. With first semester finals right around the corner, everyone is out, cutting loose on a Friday night and trying to live their best lives. Western is an academically rigorous university, and the students here like to party hard.

Apparently, I'm the only one who has zero interest in getting shitfaced or finding a hookup to go home with at the end of the night.

"Hey, Madden," a female voice coos before flattening her palms against my chest. "I haven't seen you around lately."

I blink out of those thoughts and glance down at the girl, trying to pull a name out of my ass.

Shawna something or other.

"Hey. How you doing?"

She beams and presses closer. "Better now that I've found you."

Her hands drift from my chest, past my abdominals, before pausing at the waistband of my jeans. It wouldn't surprise me if they dipped lower. Some of these girls are bold as fuck. I've come to expect it.

Although, if she decides to take the bull by the horns—so to speak—she won't be happy with what she finds.

Shawna's a gorgeous girl. Long blonde hair. Pretty face. Bright smile. Banging body.

And yet...

She's not my type.

I lift the bottle to my lips and take another sip before deciding that it's time to pull the plug on this conversation. In fact, I'm heading out. I should have known better than to come here in the first place.

Before I can do that, she nods toward a brunette who looks impatient to join our convo. "Do you see my friend over there?"

As soon as my gaze locks on the other girl, she perks up and gives me a little wave with her acrylics.

"Umm...yeah."

One hand snags the button of my jeans as the other plays with the collar of my sweatshirt before she trails her fingers down the middle of my chest. "We were thinking it'd be fun for the three of us to have a private party."

Yeah...that's not going to happen.

I clear my throat and try to come up with an excuse on the fly. "As much as I appreciate the offer, I'm gonna dip. We have a game tomorrow afternoon and I need to hit the sack." There's a beat of silence before I add, "Alone."

Her eyes widen as a mixture of confusion and disappointment morphs across her pretty features. "You're taking off without us?"

"Sorry. It's been a long week."

She forces her lower lip into a pout. "That's disappointing. Maybe another time?"

The last thing I want to do is commit.

I've seen Shawna in action. This is one girl who'll hunt me down until I make good on my promise.

"How about we play it by ear?"

Her brows pinch. "Seriously?"

"As a heart attack."

She rips her hands away and scowls. "You have no idea what you're missing out on."

A possible STI, trip to the campus clinic, and antibiotic treatment?

Yeah, I kind of do.

Shawna and her friend have been working their way through the Western Wildcats hockey roster since freshman year. And hey, I have no problem if that's what you're into, but don't get offended if I don't want to stamp my ticket and take a ride.

"You're absolutely right," I say, hoping to diffuse the situation before it can escalate any further.

Thankfully, she swings away before stomping off without drawing too much unwanted attention our way.

"What's up with that?" Riggs asks, sidling up beside me with a smirk. "Not interested in getting it on with Shawna and her friend?"

"Nah." I hoist the nearly empty bottle to my lips and drain the rest of the golden liquid. "I'm about to head out. I've had more than enough for one night."

His hand settles on my shoulder. "Bro, maybe you should consider taking her up on her offer. You need to loosen up."

I shrug.

Even though Riggs and I are close and he's a solid friend, I'm not about to confess what's really going on. Since we've returned to campus for senior year, thoughts of my ex-girlfriend have been popping into my head with more frequency than usual.

It's not like Viola has ever been far from my mind, but lately...

I keep catching flashes of her from the corner of my eye. I know damn well that my brain is playing tricks on me, but it's starting to freak me out. Especially since she attends a different university on the other side of the state. I'm not proud to admit it, but I've poured over her socials, doing my fair share of cyberstalking.

I drag a hand over my face and attempt to banish her from my thoughts for what feels like the millionth time.

We're over.

The girl wants nothing to do with me. She's shut down every attempt I've made to get back together. After three long years, I should let it go and move on with my life.

"The hottie who just walked through the door looks like a tempting treat. Long strawberry-blonde hair, big titties, and a nipped-in waist. Not to mention, she's tiny."

With a frown, I glance toward the entryway.

That description sounds suspiciously like my ex.

My gaze roams over the thick crowd. People are decked out in ugly Christmas sweaters and Santa hats. Girls have blinking light necklaces hanging loosely around their necks along with dangly ornament earrings.

As I search the sea of students, my attention gets snagged by a blonde with reddish highlights. I assume it's the one Riggs mentioned. I'm unable to catch a glimpse of her face from this angle, but she's petite. When she turns, giving me a better look at her profile, my heart trips before slamming painfully into my chest.

Full lips, pert little nose, and stubborn chin.

There's no damn way that's Viola.

But the resemblance is uncanny.

Just staring at her has a shot of electricity racing across my skin.

"Mads? Where are you going?"

Barely does Riggs' voice penetrate the thick haze clouding my brain.

"I'll be back in a sec."

I shove my way through the crowd before I can think better of it. My gaze stays locked on the girl in question as I eat up the distance between us. I'm almost afraid to see her full on because it won't be—*can't be*—Viola. And then disappointment will crash over me, sucking me to the very bottom of the ocean.

It's been three years since we saw each other in person. I'm all but starving for the sight of her. Photos haven't been nearly enough to feed the deep well of need that lives inside me.

When I'm a couple feet away, she turns, and our gazes lock. Air escapes from my lungs in a painful rush. It's like when I collide with another player on the ice and crash full force into the boards.

That's all it takes for everything to fade to the background.

I'm only cognizant of Viola.

Her eyes widen as her body stills.

Fuck.

How's it possible that she's even more beautiful than I remember?

"Vi?" My voice comes out sounding hoarse as I continue to soak her in. "What are you doing here?"

She hitches her chin and straightens her shoulders. The happiness that was flooding her features moments before vanishes. It becomes quickly apparent that as thrilled as I am to see her, she doesn't feel the same.

When she remains silent, I blurt, "Visiting your cousin?"

I met Fallyn through Vi at family gatherings. Since then, I've seen her around Western's campus. If the angry looks she shoots my way are any indication, she wishes I didn't breathe the same air as her.

Or, you know, breathe at all.

And I can't blame her for that.

"No, I go to school here now."

My brows snap together as I blink in shock. It takes a second or two for her response to sink in. "What?"

She draws in a deep breath before gradually releasing it back into the atmosphere. "I transferred to Western."

I give my head a little shake to clear the chaotic whirl of my thoughts. "When?"

"This fall."

I don't bother asking why she didn't tell me.

We both know the reason.

"Why?"

"The mechanical engineering program is better here, and they offered me a scholarship that was impossible to turn down."

But she wanted to.

It's written across her face.

She'd rather be miles and miles away from me.

Unable to help myself, I step closer. Her eyes flare as she tries to retreat but can't. We're hemmed in on all sides. It takes every bit of self-control not to reach out and yank her into my arms. It's been so long since I held her, kissed her full lips, or sank inside the welcoming heat of her body.

Fuck.

I miss it.

I miss *her*.

Did I screw other girls once I realized there was zero chance of us getting back together?

Yeah, I did. But the intimacy never came close to what it felt like to be inside Viola.

Those were more like transactions.

My ex is the only girl I've ever loved.

When it becomes obvious that she won't keep the conversational ball rolling, I add, "I haven't seen you around."

As soon as the words escape from me, I realize just how wrong I am. I *have* seen her. All those glimpses that made me question my sanity were actually her.

She jerks her shoulders in response.

My hungry gaze slides down her length, soaking in and committing every detail to memory. "You look great."

"Thanks." She rips her gaze away and glances around as if she's looking for someone to throw her a lifeline. "I should go. Fallyn's around here somewhere."

Just as she tries to slip through the crowd, I spring forward, shackling my fingers around her wrist to stop her from leaving. Her gaze drops to the place we're connected before slicing to my face.

"Can we talk?" There's a beat of silence as desperation rushes through my veins. "Please?"

Her teeth scrape across her lower lip before she shakes her head. "That's not a good idea."

"Vi..."

"I've moved on." Her expression turns frantic as she attempts to shake off my hold. "I'm sure you have as well."

When she jerks her arm for a second time, I do the only thing I can and set her free. Within seconds, she slips through the sea of bodies, disappearing completely from sight.

Pain floods my senses until it feels like I'm drowning in it.

It's only now that I've come face to face with her after years of separation and felt the gut punch of her absence that I realize there's no moving on.

There's just Vi.

3

VIOLA

"You look like you could use a drink. Maybe a few of them."

Fallyn shoves a full cup of beer into my hand. Only now do I realize that my fingers are trembling. In fact, my entire body is shaking. My knees feel weak. Any moment, they'll give out and I'll sink to the floor.

Without a word, I lift the beverage to my lips. My cousin's brows rise when I chug the contents in one thirsty gulp.

"Do you want another?"

My eyes water as I shake my head before wiping the back of my hand across my mouth. "No. That was more than enough." With any luck, it'll take the edge off.

"I'm really sorry, Vi. I didn't think he'd be here. The hockey team usually sticks to their own parties."

I release a long, slow breath. "It's fine. Who knows? Maybe it's better this way. Now I don't have to worry about running into him. It's over with."

"That's true." She chews her lower lip before her attentions settles on something just beyond my shoulder. Or, more accurately, *someone*. "Would you rather take off? We don't have to stay if you're uncomfortable."

As tempting as it is to turn around and look, I force myself to stare straight ahead.

But it's difficult.

For the past couple months, I've only caught glimpses of him across campus from a distance. To see him up close and personal was enough to steal my breath away. The Madden I knew in high school was more boyish. Three years later and he's all man. He's grown into his body. He's taller, broader in the shoulders, and more muscular. His face is more finely chiseled.

Angular.

From the moment I saw him in the hallway my freshman year of high school, I thought Madden was the most handsome boy I'd ever seen with inky colored hair that was cut longer on top and shorter on the sides. I've pushed it away from his whiskey-colored eyes a countless number of times. When my fingers itch to do it again, I tighten them and shove the memory from my brain.

"Vi?" Fallyn says, raising her voice to be heard over the music and chatter. "Are you sure you don't want to leave? It's not a big deal if you do."

I shake my head and straighten my shoulders. "No."

Even though I've spent the better part of this semester in hiding, I refuse to do it any longer. Fallyn's right. I need to live my life, and that starts tonight.

She nods toward the people shaking their asses to the beat. "Want to dance?"

"Yes." I set the empty cup down on a table and follow my cousin to the makeshift dancefloor. We wind our way through the thick press of bodies before carving out a small space for the two of us.

As much as I try to lose myself in the heavy beat of the music reverberating off the walls, it's impossible. I don't have to glance around to know that Madden is close by. I feel his eyes burning into me through the gyrating sea of students.

One song bleeds into the next as my muscles loosen. I close my eyes and tip my head upward, allowing the heavy pulse to vibrate through me. For the first time in forever, there's no longer a crushing weight resting on my shoulders, pressing me to the earth. I no longer have to skulk around campus or stay holed up in my apartment. I've dreaded what it would be like to come face to face with my ex, and that's exactly what happened tonight.

My eyelids fly open when strong hands wrap around my waist, and I find a hot blond guy in an ugly sweater and Santa hat grinning at me.

"Mind if I dance with you?"

The guy is pretty cute.

Everything inside me should be sitting up and taking notice…

Instead, there's nothing.

I force a smile. "Sure."

"You're Viola, right?"

I search his handsome face with more care. "Um, yeah. How did you know?"

He grins before laying his palm across his chest. "Ouch. I'm Matt Baker. We're in the same mechanical systems design class this semester."

"We are?"

He winces before grinning. "And the hits keep on coming."

My muscles loosen as a sheepish smile quirks my lips. "Sorry. I just transferred to Western, so I've been a little overwhelmed. Don't take it personally."

As Matt opens his mouth to respond, he's ripped away. It happens so fast that it's almost shocking. I blink only to find my ex glowering at him.

The frat guy who'd been smiling seconds ago scowls at Madden. "What's your problem, Caruso?"

"You. You're my problem," he growls, gaze flickering in my direction. "Stay the hell away from Viola. She belongs to me."

My jaw drops.

Is he serious?

I plow my hands into Madden's chest, attempting to shove him back a step. "I don't belong to you! I haven't in a while."

His eyes widen. "Vi—"

I shake my head. "You no longer have any right to interfere in my life. So do us both a favor and stay out of it."

When hot tears prick the backs of my eyes, I swing around and stalk from the living room, needing to get away from him before they fall.

4

MADDEN

Fuck!

Should I have stormed over there and ripped Matt away? Probably not.

But I couldn't bear to see another guy lay his hands on her. Even the thought of it makes me sick to my stomach.

My gaze stays fastened to Viola as she storms through the living room. It's the second time tonight she's walked away from me. Actually, she's not walking—more like running.

It's like she can't get away fast enough.

And I get it.

I hurt her.

If I were smart, I'd give her the space she so desperately wants.

But...

I've spent the past three years thinking about her and regretting how we ended. Just as she disappears out the front door, I take off, pushing through the sea of people. At least two drunk Santas get shoved out of my way. When I finally make it to the rickety porch, I slow my pace and glance around, searching the velvety darkness for Viola.

I catch sight of her on the sidewalk and burst into motion, racing down the short staircase and jogging across the yard. My feet crunch against the layer of crisp snow that blankets the grass.

Her shoulders stiffen and her pace quickens as I eat up the distance between us. "Go away, Madden."

My brain blanks. Now that I'm faced with her hurt and anger, everything I've wanted to say leaks out of my ears.

"Please, just give me five minutes."

"Why?" She wheels around and glares. "It's been three years. What's there to talk about?"

"I want to explain what happened. After I told you that I needed a little time to get my shit figured out, you refused to talk to me. You just...cut me out of your life."

Her fists settle on her hips. "What was I supposed to do? Wait around for you to decide that you wanted to be with me?" There's a pause as her eyes narrow. "I loved you more than anything and you threw away our relationship so you could screw other people."

"That's not true. It was *never* about being with other girls."

The heartache that flashes across her features makes the contents in my stomach curdle. "It doesn't matter."

I drag a hand through my hair. "That fall semester was so fucking hard. I didn't realize how tough the data analytics courses would be on top of playing hockey. Every damn second of my day was scheduled. I'd wake up, go to classes and practice, then study and hit the sheets. That was my life." I shake my head as my mind tumbles back to freshman year. "I was so overwhelmed trying to keep it all together. Most of the time, it felt like I was drowning. I never told you about it because I was embarrassed, but I bombed my first couple of exams. Coach pulled me into his office and told me that if I didn't get my grades up, I'd get benched. I already wasn't getting much play time during scrimmages. On my travel teams and in high school, I'd always been one of the best and here, I was just average. It got in my head, and I started to wonder if I even belonged at Western. On top of that, I missed the fuck out of you. All I'd wanted was a little bit of time to get everything in my life back under control again."

"That's not the way it came across. It seemed like you were pulling away so you could live your best college life and leave me behind in the past. I wanted to come for a weekend visit, and you said no. What was I supposed to think?"

"I should have explained myself better." I inch closer. It's so damn tempting to reach out and run my fingers along the curve of her jaw. I'm so hungry for the feel of her. "I should have been honest about how shitty everything was. Most of all, I'm sorry that I gave you any reason to doubt me or my love for you."

She tilts her head. "How could I not? You'd been distant for weeks and I couldn't keep going like that. It was making me sick. I had to make a clean break." The words fall from her lips like a thousand-pound stone.

My shoulders collapse under the heavy weight of her response. "If there was a way to go back and erase what happened, I'd do it in a heartbeat. I hurt the one person I cared most about. The one person I loved more than anything." I pause before whispering, "I still love you, Vi. I never stopped. Not after all these years."

Her eyes turn shiny in the silvery moonlight that slants down on us.

"So much time has slipped by. Does it even matter anymore?"

"Fuck yeah, it does," I say fiercely, swallowing up more distance between us. Even though I'm taking my life—or, at the very least, my balls—into my own hands, they settle tentatively on her shoulders. When she doesn't break the contact, I drag her closer. Her chin lifts in order to steadily hold my gaze. "In my heart, it'll always be you."

A lone tear slips down her cheek before she lowers her head and buries her face in my sweatshirt.

My arms band around her, crushing her to my chest. As soon as she's wrapped up in my strength, I squeeze my eyes tight and rest my chin against the crown of her head. There's something achingly familiar about her soft weight pressed against me.

How many times have we stood like this?

After she dumped my ass, I never thought I'd hold her again.

"Please," I whisper. "Please give me another chance. Give *us* another chance."

Need rushes through my veins as I slip my hand beneath her chin and tip it upward until I can meet her gaze. For a long moment, I search it before slowly lowering my mouth.

Once.

Twice.

Three times it ghosts over hers before finally settling. My tongue slides across the seam of her lips. All I can do is attempt to coax a response from her and see what happens.

"Let me in, baby," I whisper when her lips stay firmly pressed together.

I stroke my tongue across her mouth one last time. Just when I think she'll deny me, her lips open enough for me to steal inside. A groan rumbles up from deep within my chest as our tongues mingle and dance.

She tastes the same.

Exactly like what I remember.

Kissing Viola is like coming home, and it only makes me more determined to win her back.

I lose track of how long our mouths stay fused together. We only break apart when a car whizzes past, honking obnoxiously before some asshole shouts out the window, "Get a room!"

We're both breathing hard as I rest my forehead against hers and stare into her eyes.

"Will you at least think about giving me a second chance?"

When her tongue darts out to moisten her lips, as if she's trying to taste me there, another groan of need rumbles up from within.

"I don't know." There's a long pause. "I'll think about it."

Air empties from my lungs.

It's more than I could have hoped for.

She shivers as we break away, and I quickly yank my Western Wildcats sweatshirt off before dragging it over her head and down her torso. A deep sense of satisfaction fills me at the sight of her wearing something that's mine. There used to be a time when she begged prettily to wear my sweatshirts or jerseys.

And I loved it.

Everyone who glanced at Viola knew who she belonged to. My name was stamped across her back for all to see.

She burrows into the warmth of the cotton. "Won't you be cold?"

I shrug. "Nah, I'm fine. I practically live at the arena. I'm used to it by now." Even though I don't want this night to end, it's better to leave it on a good note than continue to press my luck.

"Come on. I'll walk you home." Plus, I can figure out where she lives.

Her teeth scrape across her lower lip before she finally agrees. "Okay."

Arousal hits me like a punch to the gut as we fall in line and continue walking. It's the most I've felt in years.

"You know it kills me when you do that, right?"

She gives me a bit of side eye as a smile twitches around the corners of her lips. "Yeah, I do."

Vi always did know how to drive me crazy.

Even though it feels like everything has changed between us, it's comforting to see that some things are still the same.

5

VIOLA

There's a knock on my bedroom door before Fallyn peeks her head around the corner of it. "Are you awake?"

With a groan, I glance at the clock on the nightstand. It's not even seven in the morning. "If I wasn't before, I am now," I grumble. "What are you doing up so early? It's Saturday. You're supposed to sleep in. Isn't it a rule or something?"

Unperturbed by my grouchy disposition, a smile springs to her lips as she pushes open the door and beelines to the bed before dropping down beside me. I truly don't understand how she can be so bright-eyed and bushytailed after a night of partying.

Barely am I able to crack open my eyelids.

And my butt was home by eleven.

Although, I did spend most of the night tossing and turning, thinking about Madden.

And the kiss we shared.

The memory is enough to make my belly tremble.

I've made out with a number of guys since our breakup, but none were able to rouse the kind of feelings he does. Over the years, I've done my best to convince myself that my memories were faulty.

That's no longer possible.

In fact, his kisses are even better than I remember.

How's that for a kick in the pants?

"What happened to you last night?" The smile disappears as she shoots me a frown. "You better not have walked home by yourself."

Oh boy.

Fallyn will probably flip out when I tell her the truth. And I can't blame her for it. She was the one who listened to me cry on the phone after we broke up. She's the one who dropped everything and came to stay at our house. She arrived on the doorstep with chocolate, mood music, and a list of our favorite movies to marathon.

The other option would be to lie, and I refuse to do that. Not only are we cousins, but besties as well. Moving in with her this semester has been the one bright spot in transferring to Western.

"I didn't." There's a moment of hesitation before I force out the rest. "Madden walked me home."

Her brows shoot up, nearly crashing into her hairline. "Please tell me that you met another Madden last night and we're not talking about your ex."

With a wince, I mumble, "I can't do that."

She groans before staring up at the ceiling. "Vi!"

"I know, okay? I know."

"Did you kiss him?"

"I'm going to plead the fifth on that one."

She swears under her breath before flopping onto the bed so that we're lying side by side. "Look, I know how much you love him—"

"Loved," I say, correcting her.

She swivels her face to meet my gaze before giving me a steely look. "You can try to fool me, but please don't lie to yourself."

Ouch.

Unfortunately, she's not wrong.

If last night showed me anything, it's that I'm still in love with him.

Just as she opens her mouth, there's a knock on the apartment door. We both glance toward the hallway as she springs from the bed.

"That's probably the bagels and coffee I ordered."

She disappears from the room. When a couple minutes tick by and Fallyn doesn't return, my belly growls and I decide to head to the kitchen. Bagels and coffee sounds like the breakfast of champions. I grab the sweatshirt lying haphazardly on my desk chair before dragging it over my head. It's only when it settles around me that I realize it's the sweatshirt Madden gave me last night.

Unable to help myself, I lift the material to my nose and inhale a deep breath. As soon as the woodsy aroma teases my senses, a wave of nostalgia crashes over me and I squeeze my eyes tightly closed. I never imagined that seeing him, talking to him...*kissing him* would unlock so many memories. Not only the brutal pain of our breakup but all the good times as well.

My fingers settle at the hem of the material. I'm about to yank it off when there's a light knock on the bedroom door.

"Vi?"

I glance at Fallyn, who hovers at the threshold. "Yeah?"

Her lips are pressed into a tight line. "Madden's here."

My eyes widen as I point to the carpet beneath my bare feet. "He's *here*? Now?"

"Yeah, and he wants to talk." She perks up. "Should I tell him to go fuck himself?"

I snort at the mental image that question conjures. Fallyn would love nothing more than to tear into my ex.

With her teeth.

"No, send him in."

She jerks a brow. "Are you sure that's a good idea?"

Of course it isn't.

"Yeah." I pause for a heartbeat before adding, "I'll be fine."

Instead of arguing, she says, "I know you will."

She vanishes from the hallway before I can rethink my decision.

Barely do I get a chance to suck in a shaky breath and calm everything raging within when Madden appears in the doorway. "Hey, Vi. Is it all right if I come in?"

With a nod, I cross my arms against my chest. His gaze drops to the movement, and I see the moment he realizes I'm wearing his sweatshirt.

I clear my throat, only wanting to get this convo over with. "What are you doing here?"

He inches further into the room before glancing around the space. The queen-sized bed is still rumpled and my clothing from last night is in a small pile near the closet. Engineering books are stacked neatly on my desk and posters of the Eiffel Tower and the Louvre decorate the walls. I took a school trip to Paris when I was in eighth grade, and it left a lasting impression. There's a collage of pictures that date back to elementary school. He gravitates toward the board. If he's expecting to find any hint of him in my past, he won't. I made sure there wasn't a trace left.

Sadness fills his eyes as he studies the photos.

Before I can ask for a second time why he's here, he swivels around.

His whiskey-colored eyes skewer me in place. "I have a proposition for you."

My brows rise as I tilt my head. "What are you talking about?"

"Give me twenty-four hours to show you what it could be like between us. I'm not the same guy I was at eighteen. Just like you, I've grown and matured." When I remain silent, he takes a step closer. "If you give me a fair shot and decide you want nothing to do with me, I won't bother you again."

There's a part within my brain that's screaming for me to shut down this dangerous conversation.

Just spending thirty minutes in his presence last night was difficult.

But...

Maybe that's exactly what I need.

To test myself and prove once and for all that I'm over it.

And how better to do that than spend time with him?

"Vi?"

His soft voice knocks me from the whirl of my thoughts.

"Okay." The response escapes before I can think better of it.

Surprise flickers in his eyes. "Really?"

I jerk my head into a nod. "Yeah. But just remember what you promised. At the end of twenty-four hours, if I decide you're better off in my past, that's where I want you to stay."

He straightens to his full height and stalks closer. My breath catches at the back of my throat as I lift my chin to hold his gaze. "I really hope that won't be your decision."

I retreat, needing more distance between us. It feels like I'm suffocating. "It will be."

"Challenge accepted."

"What happens now?"

He rips his gaze away long enough to slip his phone from the pocket of his sweatpants before glancing at it. "I need to get to the arena. We have a game this afternoon and I'd like you there."

I swallow the painful lump that has settled in my throat. I can't count the number of times I sat in the bleachers and watched Madden on the ice. Not only for games, but practices as well.

"Okay."

"I need to head over there, but I'll have a ticket waiting for you. Do you want to bring Fallyn?"

"I'll ask, but I'm not sure if she'll go. She's not exactly your number-one fan."

"Yeah, I figured that out already. She had a lot to say when she opened the door and found me on the other side."

For the first time since he entered the room, my lips hitch into a reluctant smile. "I'll bet."

"I'll see you after the game."

It's only when he disappears into the hallway that I release the pent-up breath in my lungs.

Not more than fifteen seconds pass before my cousin bursts into the room. "Are you seriously going to spend the next twenty-four hours with that guy?"

My mouth tumbles open. "Did you stand outside the door and listen to our entire conversation?"

She cocks a brow. "Did you really think I wouldn't?"

Well...she's got me there.

6

VIOLA

We stop at the concession stand on the way inside the arena and grab two big pretzels and bottles of water before making our way to our seats. I glance at the tickets and realize that they're at center ice near the glass. That was always my favorite place to watch a game.

As we settle in, the Zamboni finishes up and rolls into the garage before the metal door slides down. Both teams jump onto the ice, circling around their half for warmups.

"Are you sure you want to go through with this?" Fallyn asks, ripping off a piece of warm pretzel. "It's not too late to change your mind. We could always bail and then take out a restraining order."

With a snort, my gaze slides across the players before zeroing in on Madden. He's wearing the same number from high school.

Forty-four.

"I don't think that's necessary, do you?"

"Maybe. I haven't decided yet."

As he turns the corner and skates in my direction, his gaze fastens onto mine. If I'd thought a little bit of distance this morning would give me some much-needed perspective, that doesn't happen. As the lights in the arena are dimmed, the players from the opposing team are announced and then the same is done with the Wildcats roster. The crowd cheers and claps, hooting and whistling for fan favorites. A small thrill shoots through me when Madden's name is called, and he glides onto the ice. Even though it's dark, his gaze remains locked on mine.

As much as I want to drag my attention from him, that's impossible.

Ever since we started dating, Madden was my entire world.

My life revolved around him.

When he was a senior, we'd talk about how great it would be when I joined him at Western.

And then...

I shake those thoughts away as the puck gets dropped at center ice and the Wildcats quickly take possession. It doesn't take long before I'm immersed in the game. I've always enjoyed watching Madden play hockey. Only now do I realize how much I've missed it. Even my cousin is reluctantly sucked into the action. We both jump to our feet and cheer when the Wildcats score a goal.

By the third period, both pretzels have been devoured and I'm sitting on the edge of my seat. The game is tied and has turned into a real barn burner with only two minutes left. Tension and excitement continues to build throughout the arena.

When there's less than a minute left in the period, Madden's teammate passes the puck to him, and he makes a drive for the net. As a defenseman closes in, he passes it to another wing before the small black disc is slid back to Madden, who dekes out the same player and rips off a shot.

My breath catches at the back of my throat as I rise to my feet. It all happens in slow motion. The goalie slides but isn't quick enough to catch the puck that whizzes past him. The black rubber disc hits the back of the net and everyone around me goes crazy. A horn blares, signaling a goal as the clock runs out.

The Wildcats pull off a win.

As Madden's teammates slap him on the back, congratulating

him, his gaze stays pinned to mine. He raises his arm and points to me.

With that, a little more distance falls away.

"I can already tell how tonight is going to go," Fallyn mutters.

As much as I want to reassure her that there's nothing to worry about, I can't.

She has every right to be concerned.

And so do I.

7

MADDEN

"Why are you in such a hurry to get out of here?" Wolf asks as I throw on a sweatshirt and run my hands through my hair.

I give him a bit of side eye. We've known each other since freshman year. What happened with Fallyn's family was total shit, but I've never let that skew my opinion of him. Not only is Wolf my roommate, he's turned out to be a good friend. But here's the thing—he doesn't realize I know about his past. He isn't aware that Fallyn's cousin was my girlfriend at the time.

After the breakup, there didn't seem much point in bringing it up.

"My ex goes to school here now," I say carefully, realizing that if my relationship with Viola goes any further, I'll have to come clean.

When he nods, I continue. "I'm taking her out, and I guess we'll see what happens."

Even though I try to play it off, nerves are eating me from the inside out.

He smirks before stepping closer and gently slapping my cheek. "Aww, my boy is finally going out on a date. Do we need to have a little talk about the birds and bees?"

I snort. "You're half a dozen years too late for that." There's a pause before I admit, "Although, it's been a while."

"Yeah, I was beginning to wonder if you'd taken a vow of chastity or something. Maybe became a born-again virgin."

He's not wrong.

It's been a while.

We're talking years.

Years.

Let that sink in.

Once I realized that Viola had cut me out of her life, I attempted to drown myself in the groupies who constantly buzz around the team. It didn't take long to figure out that if I couldn't have her, I didn't want anyone else.

"Nah. Just waiting for the right girl to come back around."

"Well, good luck." His joking manner falls away. "I hope it works out."

Yeah, me too.

The last thing I want to do is get my hopes up.

Only now am I wondering if I've shot myself in the foot by giving Viola an easy out. If we spend the next twenty hours together and she decides it's truly over, there's nothing I can do about it.

I gave her my word, and I refuse to break it.

I draw a deep breath into my lungs before gradually releasing it back into the atmosphere. I need to pull out all the stops and make it a night she'll remember.

There's nothing more I can do.

"Thanks, man."

With that, I grab my coat and head for the locker room door, impatient to see Vi again.

As soon as I step into the lobby, my gaze coasts over the crowd of parents, girlfriends, and fans until it lands on Viola. And just like always, my heart jackhammers a mad rhythm. Ever since I first laid eyes on her, that's the way it's been and nothing—not three long years—has changed it. I never imagined getting a second chance.

Brody McKinnon, Maverick's father, claps me on the back as I pass by. "Nice goal at the end of the game."

"Thanks, Mr. McKinnon."

He glances at Viola and shoots me a smile. "Looks like someone's waiting for you."

My lips quirk. "An old friend."

He pats me again as Maverick and Ryder McAdams join the group. "Have a good night."

"We will."

Viola's gaze stays locked on mine as I swallow up the distance that separates us.

When I'm close enough, she says, "That was a great game."

"Thanks. I always played better when you were watching." I glance around, looking for her cousin. "Did Fallyn take off?"

"Yeah. She didn't want to stick around."

Even though she doesn't mention it, I think that has more to do with Wolf than me.

When the conversation stalls, I clear my throat. "Did you enjoy the game?"

"Actually, I did." There's a pause before she admits, "It's been a while since I've attended one. I forgot how much fun they are."

"Good. I'm glad you came to watch."

"Me, too."

I jerk my head toward the exit. "Ready to get out of here?"

"Yup."

The chilly breeze slides over our cheeks as we step outside. When we're close enough to my SUV, I click the locks and pop open the passenger side door. Once she slides inside, I hustle around the hood and settle on the leather seat next to her. One punch of the button and the engine leaps to life. I give it a minute or two to warm up before pulling onto the tree-lined street near campus.

"I thought we could head downtown and walk around a little bit." I watch her from the corner of my eye to get a read on her reaction. "I remember how much you used to enjoy the lights at Christmas."

Our gazes catch for just a second before I rip mine away and stare out the windshield. It would be all too easy to drown in her green depths.

"That sounds fun."

"Is there something else you'd rather do instead?" I ask quickly.

"No. It'll be nice to walk around after sitting in the stands."

"Then, maybe, we can grab dinner." I hate how tentative everything feels between us. It never used to be that way.

"Sure."

It's only when I've secured her agreement do my muscles loosen. The closer we get to the center of town, the more congested traffic becomes. Since it's crowded, I park on a side street that's a block away. We exit the vehicle and meet at the front of the hood before I hold out my hand. She stares at it for a heartbeat or two before hesitantly placing her fingers in mine. A shot of electricity zips through me at the contact.

With our hands clasped, we head to the stoplight on the corner. Vi's eyes widen as she catches a glimpse of the illuminations. Every year, the city strings lights outside each building until they're covered.

"Wow. It's so beautiful," she says, voice filled with wonder.

"Yeah, it is." Once I had my license in high school, we'd drive through the neighborhoods and admire the lights. It became a tradition. After the breakup, I couldn't bring myself to look at Christmas decorations. All it did was remind me of the girl I'd lost.

We spend the next hour or so walking up one side of the street before crossing over and strolling down the other. She points out an ice statue in the shape of a Christmas tree. There are sculpted blocks outside every business. The entire time we meander, I keep her hand firmly ensconced in my own.

Being with her is like tumbling back in time.

We peruse the stores and Vi buys a couple small gifts for her parents. When our bellies begin to growl, we decide to stop for dinner at a small Italian restaurant. The hostess seats us at a table for two near a large picture window with a perfect view of the street.

It's amazing how much better everything feels when we're together.

Once we've plowed our way through our dinners—lasagna for her, spaghetti and meatballs for me—I spring my plans on her for the rest of the evening.

"I was thinking we could book a room at the hotel down the street and spend the night." When she goes still, I blurt, "Just to sleep. And talk. I don't have any other expectations."

Vi glances down at her plate before asking softly, "Do you think that's a good idea?"

I press closer to the table, hating the distance between us. "I really enjoyed having you at the game and just walking around, looking at the lights tonight. It reminds me of how it used to be, and I don't want it to end." Then I tack on the clincher. "You promised to give me twenty-four hours."

"And you agreed to leave me alone if that's what I decide," she fires back.

Even though I probably should have expected it, her response is like a knife through the heart. Any moment, I'll bleed out.

I dip my head in acknowledgment. "I'll stick to my word if you do the same."

She notches her chin. "I will."

When the waiter stops by our table to ask if either of us would like dessert, I glance at Vi and she shakes her head. I hand over a credit card without looking at the check. After the bill is taken care of, I slip my arm around Vi and steer her out the restaurant door.

We stop at the Kris Kringle pop-up market that sells homemade gifts, spiced cider, and candy. Another hour slides by before we arrive at the Wiltshire Hotel. My parents stayed here last year when they came to visit for the weekend, so I know it's a nice place.

Her breath catches as we step inside the lobby. It's all marble and dark wood with crystal chandeliers hanging from the double story ceiling. There are cozy seating arrangements near a fireplace at the far end of the space.

The hotel is high end and screams money. Which is something I don't have a ton of since I play hockey during the school year and can only work during the summer. I don't give a damn what tonight costs. Viola is worth it.

Spending time alone with her is worth it.

As we head to the reservation desk, an eight-foot-tall gingerbread house catches our attention.

I nod toward the roped-off decoration. "Do you want to check it out while I see if there are any rooms available?"

"Sure."

"I'll be over in a minute."

My gaze stays glued to her for a second or two before I head to the reception desk. The lady behind the counter tells me that there's only one king-sized room available in the entire place. She confides that a lot of guests are staying in town for the weekend, enjoying the Christmas festivities. As soon as she hands over the key cards, I beeline toward Vi. She's snapping a few photos with her phone.

The gingerbread house glitters with fluffy white frosting piped around the eves and oversized gumdrops on the rooftop. Lights have been strung on the outside with red and green clothed elves that hang out of the windows. There are Christmas trees decorated with more lights and big, colorful balls.

"This is really cool. I've never seen anything like it before." She cranes her neck to peek through the open door. A soft light illuminates the inside, showing more elves and candy. "Did you know that they have a gingerbread house in the lobby every year?"

"I saw it when my parents stayed here. It made me think of you."

When she gives me a speculative look, I shrug. "Christmas used to be your favorite time of year, and I wanted to do something you'd enjoy."

She glances again at the house. "It still is." There's a pause before she adds, "Thank you."

"You're welcome."

We take our time, walking around the perimeter, pointing out all the little details.

After fifteen minutes, I pop the question that's been circling through my brain. "Are you ready to go upstairs?"

8
VIOLA

My belly dips as I glance at Madden before jerking my head into a tight nod. I have no idea why I'm so nervous about being alone with him. It's certainly not the first time. Maybe I'm afraid that the walls I've been trying so hard to hold in place are going to crumble. Already, I feel him steadily wearing away at my defenses.

When he offers his outstretched hand, I slip my fingers into it and a little zip of electricity sizzles in the air around us. I hate just how right it feels.

How right *he* feels.

With clasped hands, we head to the elevator. Once the doors slide open, we step inside, and Madden presses the button for the fourth floor. My gaze settles on our reflection in the mirrored walls that surround us.

It's a little surreal.

"Are you all right?" he asks quietly.

My attention arrows to him in the mirror. Concern swims in his eyes. "Yeah, I'm fine." My tongue darts out to moisten my lips before I tack on, "This is just...*weird*."

He pops a brow. "You think so?"

With a shrug, I glance away. "After how we ended, I never expected this."

When he remains silent, I force my eyes back to his in the mirror.

His shoulders collapse as he whispers, "I just wanted to spend time with you, but maybe this wasn't the right way to do it. If you'd rather end this now, we can part ways and I won't bother you again."

My eyes widen.

That's not the response I was expecting.

"Really?"

He plows a hand through his mahogany-colored short strands. "Yeah. The last thing I want to do is make you uncomfortable. After the game, dinner, and walking around for a couple of hours, if you don't want to spend more time with me, it's unlikely anything else will change your mind." His voice dips. "Maybe you're right and there isn't a way for us to move forward. No matter how much I want it. Because you have to want it too."

I release a slow breath as some of my anxiety falls away.

Is that what I want?

To walk away from Madden and put him firmly in the past?

It's almost a surprise to realize that I'm not ready for tonight to end. I have no idea what the future holds for us, but I need to spend more time with him in order to figure it out.

When I remain silent, he says, "Vi?"

Our gazes cling. "I'll stay."

His brows rise as if he was expecting a different response. It's funny...a couple of hours ago, I would have taken the first out he gave me.

"Really?"

I nod. "Yeah."

A slow smile lights up his face. It's enough to have my belly doing a somersault.

"I'm glad. Tonight's been fun."

"It has."

The doors slide open, and his fingers slip around mine before he tugs me into the hallway. He glances at a gold plaque on the wall filled with room numbers and then swings to the left. We turn down a long stretch of hallway before stopping in front of a gleaming black painted door. Madden swipes the key and the door buzzes, a green light flickering before he pushes open the thick wood. I slip past him before stepping into the room.

Except…it's not just a room.

More like a small apartment but way fancier than anything I've ever seen. There's a tiny entryway with an antique credenza and a crystal bowl. A gold leaf framed mirror hangs above it. My gaze roams over the space as I walk further into the suite. A compact kitchenette is to the left and a spacious sitting area with a fireplace and pretty mantle painted in antique white takes up a good portion of the far wall.

But what draws my attention is the floor-to-ceiling windows that overlook the entire downtown area. I can't help but gravitate to the large expanse of glass and the lights that illuminate the street below.

"It's breathtaking," I whisper, my face pressed against the window.

"I can honestly say I've never seen anything more beautiful."

The deep timbre of his voice has me turning to meet his eyes. He's not looking at downtown.

He's staring at me.

My mouth turns cottony. I force myself to say, "This place is way too expensive. I can't imagine how much you spent."

He shrugs. "No matter what you decide tomorrow, spending time alone with you was worth it. That's all you need to know."

His earnest words make my heart swell. It's exactly what I was afraid of, but there doesn't seem to be anything I can do to stop it from happening.

I glance toward the French doors across from the fireplace before stepping toward them and peeking inside. The bedroom is spacious with a king-sized bed that dominates most of the area, along with a table and two armchairs parked near the expansive window. Curious to explore, I wander into the massive bathroom. It's all gray veined marble with a giant soaker tub and oversized waterfall shower. Just like in the living area, there's a wall of windows with spectacular views of downtown.

"I was thinking you might like a bath. I remember how much you used to enjoy them."

I still do.

There's just not a chance for me to indulge as often as I'd like. The bathroom at the apartment is tiny. It's utilitarian at best.

I chew my lower lip and stare at the tub.

A few thick white candles in gleaming silver holders are scattered around the space. I can just imagine darkening the room, lighting the candles, and relaxing in a bath while staring at the city below.

"Or we could just—"

"No, I'd really like that."

He nods, crossing to the tub and turning on the faucet before testing the water. Once the temperature has been adjusted, he beelines to the counter and looks through a couple of drawers until he finds an igniter and lights the candles, placing them around the ledge of the tub before hitting the switch so that the room is plunged into darkness.

A discrete knock on the outside door interrupts the silence that's fallen over us.

Madden jerks his head toward the bedroom. "I'll be back in a couple of minutes."

Before I can ask any questions, he closes the door behind him. When the porcelain tub is about halfway filled, I strip off my clothing. Each garment that gets removed is folded and neatly placed on the counter before I step into the water. A hiss of air escapes from my lips as I slowly stretch out until warmth laps at my collarbone.

My eyelids flutter closed as I draw a deep breath into my lungs and gradually release it back into the atmosphere. Just when my mind begins to wander and it feels as if I'll drift into a light slumber, there's a soft knock on the bathroom door.

"Is it all right if I come in?"

My eyelids spring open. "Of course."

It's not like Madden hasn't seen me naked before. We spent years together.

He walks in with a bottle of champagne in one hand and two crystal flutes in the other. The cork has already been popped. He sets the glasses on the counter and carefully pours golden bubbly liquid in each one.

"I thought you might like something to drink."

I straighten in the tub, my fingers wrapping around the delicate stem before bringing the rim to my lips and taking a sip.

Madden settles on the edge of the tub. His gaze stays locked on mine as he brings the flute to his lips and takes a swallow. The corded muscles of his throat constrict. The movement is unexpectedly sexy.

"I hope at the very least, we can be friends after this."

While we dated, Madden was my best friend. But we were never platonic. There was always something more between us.

"Vi?"

I shake my head. "I'm not sure if that's possible."

Can I spend time with him and not want more?

I think it would be too painful to see him with other girls.

It's the reason I went to such great lengths to avoid him after the breakup. I was never one to stalk his social media. I didn't want to know what he was up to. I didn't want those images seared into my brain for all eternity.

He looks down at the flute in his hand and swirls the remaining liquid. "There's never been a day that I haven't regretted how we ended. It'll haunt me for the rest of my life."

It takes effort to blink back the wetness that stings my eyes. Three years later and the past still has the power to wound me. It would be so much easier to deal with if I were over it.

Over him.

Maybe if I'd moved on with someone else...

But that didn't happen.

Deep down in a place I've been loath to acknowledge, it's always been Madden.

My greatest fear is that no other man will be able to carve out even a small place in my heart, and I'll be doomed to compare every guy to him and ultimately find them lacking.

I drag my gaze away to stare out at the city below us. I never imagined feeling this conflicted. Only now do I realize that I've been fooling myself. Just because I pretended my feelings for him were dead and buried doesn't mean they were.

Now, the question is—what am I going to do about it?

What do I *want* to do about it?

Instead of continuing the conversation, he asks, "Should I add more water to the tub?"

I shake my head. "No, I'm ready to get out."

When he rises to his feet, I do the same. Water sluices off my warmed flesh and a tortured groan rumbles up from deep within his chest as his gaze licks over every inch of my naked form.

"It might not seem like it, but I really am trying to do the right thing here."

"I know."

His voice deepens. "You're not making it easy."

It's almost a surprise when he swings away and sets his glass down before grabbing a white towel from the silver rack. Returning, he holds out the plush cotton.

His gaze roams over my length. "Here. Use this to dry off."

"Will you do it for me?"

"Vi..."

"Please?"

It's been such a long time since he's touched my body, and I crave the sensation of his strong hands stroking over me.

Even if there's a towel between us.

His expression turns conflicted as he remains still. For a heartbeat or two, I wonder if he'll turn me down.

"Is that what you really want?"

"It is." Only now do I realize just how true those words are.

With that, he extends his hand to assist me from the tub.

9

MADDEN

What the hell am I doing?

If I lay one finger on her, I'll be lost.

Fuck...I'm already lost.

The moment I caught sight of her at the party last night, it was game over.

My hands shake as I gently run the thick cotton over the slope of her shoulders and then along her bare arms. There've been so many nights since our breakup that I imagined touching her like this.

Not one damn time did I think I'd be given the chance to make things right between us. It's almost a mindfuck to have her so close and not know if it'll go beyond tomorrow morning. If she walks away, it'll probably crush me. Which is exactly why I need to play this right and not push for too much.

My heart thrashes against my ribcage as I slide the material down her collarbone to her breasts. Vi has always been a handful, but she's even more so now. She has an hourglass figure.

Curvy and generous.

The sight of her naked would be enough to bring any man to his knees.

Her nipples tighten as I gently brush the cotton over them.

My cock turns painfully hard, throbbing with need. Any moment, I'll go off like a shot.

How embarrassing would that be?

It's not something that's happened since the beginning of our relationship when we held off on having sex. Even back then, I didn't want to push Vi into something she wasn't ready for.

My hands drift to her belly as I sink to my knees so that I'm eye level with her core. Unlike when we were in high school, her pussy is shaved bare and it's like a shot straight to my dick. Her fragrance slyly wraps around me, cocooning me in the past, and I sway closer before inhaling a deep breath.

It's only when I've wrestled my baser instincts under control that I slant my eyes upward and meet her gaze.

"Should I stop?"

The best thing would be for her to dry herself off, but she silently shakes her head as her teeth nip her lower lip.

I release a steady breath and fight for control before stroking the towel up and down her legs, drying off her feet before making my way back up her body until I reach her plush lips.

"Sit on the edge of the tub." The command shoots out of my mouth before I can stop it.

She doesn't hesitate.

"Do you want me to dry that sweet little pussy?"

Her breath catches and her cheeks pinken. "Yes."

"Then spread your legs for me."

Just like before, she follows my direction and widens her thighs until I'm treated to a full view of her soft pink center.

Fuck.

Another groan rumbles up from my chest and breaks the silence of the room.

She's so damn beautiful.

I take my time, eating her up with my eyes. After I've looked my fill, I drag the cottony material from the top of her slit to the bottom before slowly running it back to her clit. Her eyes dilate as she whimpers, spreading her legs further.

"That feels so good," she whispers.

I repeat the movement, wanting to give her as much pleasure as possible. She braces her palms on the marble ledge and arches her back. Everything inside me swells as her lips turn slick with arousal. My gaze stays fastened to her pussy as my mouth waters for a taste of her sweetness.

"How long has it been?" As much as I don't want to know, I *need* to know.

She wiggles closer as I continue to swipe the towel over her soaked flesh.

"Almost a year."

"It's been two for me," I admit.

She cracks open her eyelids to meet my gaze. "Really?"

"It didn't take long to realize that if I couldn't have you, I didn't want anyone else."

Softness floods her expression. "I felt the same. No one else wiped away your memory."

Another groan escapes from her as I drop the towel to the tile floor and run my fingers over her delicate flesh before slipping one thick digit inside her heat.

"Madden..." Her voice turns tortured.

"All you have to do is tell me to stop and I'll do it."

I draw my finger out of her before circling her clit with the pad of my thumb. Even though I was only in high school when we started having sex, I devoured everything I could find online about pleasing a woman.

Her pleasure always came before my own.

She shakes her head and widens her legs even more. "I want you to make me come."

"You need to be sure, Vi. I don't want to be a mistake you regret in the morning. It would kill me."

"That's not going to happen."

A battle gets waged inside me before I finally give in. "How do you want to come? Fingers or tongue?"

"I want your tongue. It's always been my favorite."

A smirk quirks my lips. "I remember how much you enjoyed my mouth on you, and I loved doing it."

When she cries out at the first lash, I run the flat of my tongue over her slit. The taste of her honey explodes in my mouth, filling my senses.

"That feels so good."

"Not nearly as good as you taste."

Fuck, but I've missed this.

I've missed everything about Viola.

Every.

Damn.

Thing.

I thrust my tongue deep inside her before nibbling at her clit. It doesn't take long for her body to tighten in response. Another leisurely lap is all it takes to push her over the precipice and into oblivion.

I continue licking her pussy as she moans out her orgasm. It's only when her muscles turn lax that I press a kiss against her clit before drawing away and searching her face for signs of remorse.

When I find none, I pop to my feet before grabbing the neatly folded robe on the marble counter and wrapping it around her naked body. I sweep her up into my arms and carry her to the king-sized bed in the other room. Shifting her around, I draw back the covers and carefully set her down before stripping to my boxers and slipping beneath the sheets. Then, I pull her into my arms and hold her tight.

It doesn't take long for her breathing to even out.

A few minutes later, I follow her into slumber.

10

VIOLA

A deep sense of wellbeing fills me as I wake with a stretch and immediately come into contact with a hard body. My eyelids spring open as my brain somersaults.

What the—

That's when the previous twenty-four hours crash back into my brain.

Madden.

I watched his hockey game—something I haven't done since high school—and then we held hands and walked around downtown, had dinner, and ended up at a pricey hotel with amazing views over the city.

He ran me a bath, and I relaxed in the deliciously hot water while drinking a flute of chilled champagne. After that, he dried me off and licked me until I shattered into a million broken pieces.

It had felt even better than when we were together in high school.

And then he carried me to the bed where we fell asleep.

"I hope you're not already having regrets."

His deep voice breaks into the whirl of my thoughts, and I twist my head until my gaze can fasten onto his. As soon as it does, a sizzle of awareness shoots through me, electrifying my insides.

"Nope." It's only after the answer escapes from my lips that I realize it's the truth. I don't regret spending the day with him or the way he touched me.

And yet...

I have no idea how we move forward.

Unable to help myself, my gaze rakes over his features. The softness of youth has melted away, leaving a handsome man in its place. I don't realize that I've reached out to cup his cheek until he presses it into my palm.

"I still love you, Vi. I never stopped."

I release a shaky breath and admit the truth. "I love you, too."

Tension gathers in the lines of his face. "But?"

"If we're really going to do this, we need to take it slow. It's going to take time to build back the trust between us."

He turns his face until his lips can graze the flesh of my palm. "All I'm asking for is a chance. Can you give me that?"

The question circles through my head.

"Yeah." As he tugs me into his arms, I whisper, "But I don't think I could bear it if you hurt me again."

He presses a kiss against the crown of my head. "I won't. Promise."

My body gradually melts against his. Madden has always been muscular, but he's so much harder now than he was in high school. I shove the blankets back in order to get a good look at him. He had the chance last night to eat me up with his eyes, but I wasn't given the same opportunity.

And I want it.

I want to explore every inch of him.

I want to reacquaint myself with his body.

My fingers glide across his chest before drifting over the grooved ridges of his abdomen. He's still wearing boxer briefs. The thick robe he'd wrapped around me after the bath disappeared during the night, leaving me naked against the high-thread-count sheets.

I tug the elastic band of his boxers. "Take them off."

"Vi..." His deep voice trails off on a groan. "It's important we take our time and not move too quickly."

"You're right." I snap the band against his taut flesh. "But I want to touch you the same way you touched me last night."

"I don't want you to regret—"

"I won't. You haven't done anything that I didn't want. If I decide to pump the breaks and take a couple steps back, I'll tell you."

He nods. "Just know you're the one in charge."

I straighten as he slips the briefs down his thighs until his erection can spring free.

His cock is thick and long. The first time I caught a glimpse of it, I didn't think there was any way it would fit inside me, but I was wrong. Before we finally slept together, I spent hours petting him, playing with it, sucking the blunt-tipped head into my mouth. He was so careful the first time we had sex, treating me like spun glass. I couldn't imagine our experience being more perfect.

When he reclines against the mattress, my gaze drifts over him. His body is a work of art, sculpted from lifting weights and playing hockey.

My fingers follow the path of my gaze. They glide over his chest and then abdominals before finally arriving at his cock. Heat floods my core as I inch closer to that part of him. Already there's a pearly drop beading the slit. I run my fingers from the tip, down his shaft, before cupping his balls. As I squeeze them, a guttural groan rumbles up from his chest and he arches into my hand.

Unable to resist for another moment, I lean toward him and flick my tongue over the mushroom-shaped head before sucking him deep inside my mouth.

His fingers tangle in my hair. "Fuck, baby, that feels so good."

I didn't realize how much I missed touching him, kissing and licking him, until now.

When his body tightens, he gently pushes me away. My eyes flicker to his in confusion as he shakes his head. Straightening, he slips his arms around my ribs before hauling me on top of him.

His mouth settles over mine as he whispers, "You don't need to do that."

"I want to."

"I know but I think it's best if we take this slow."

I nip at his lower lip before sucking the fullness into my mouth. When fire ignites in his eyes, I release it with a soft pop and reposition myself to straddle his pelvis.

"Vi...I'm serious," he growls as his cock turns impossibly hard.

I rub my pussy along his thick shaft. The movement has my eyes rolling to the back of my head.

"I want to feel you inside me. It's been too long since you've filled me up."

"You need to stop saying those kinds of things or I'm going to lose it."

When I slide against him for a second time, he flexes his hips and slips deep inside my heat.

Tortured groans escape from both of us.

"Fuck. Are you still on the pill?"

I nod.

His teeth graze his lower lip as his brow furrows. "I didn't bring any condoms with me. I didn't think we'd need them."

"It's all right. I have one in my purse."

If the comment surprises him, it doesn't show on his face. Even though I was adamant nothing would happen between us, I wanted to be safe rather than sorry.

I rise to my knees until only the tip of his cock is inside me. "Should I get it?"

It's slowly that I slide down his length.

"Yeah." His voice is raw and filled with need.

After a few more pumps, I slip from him and race to the living area where I tossed my purse last night. I rifle through the contents before finding the rubber in a small side pocket. As soon as my fingers grasp it, I swing around and retrace my steps.

I rip open the foil packet with my teeth before kneeling on the bed and pulling out the condom. The latex gets placed over the tip of his cock and carefully rolled to the root. Once he's completely covered, I straddle him for a second time. With one hand, I guide him back inside my body before sinking all the way down.

A whimper of pleasure escapes from my lips.

No one has ever felt as good as Madden. I spent the past three years trying to convince myself that he didn't matter or what we had wasn't special, but it was a lie.

Pleasure reverberates throughout my entire being. Every thrust of his hips sends shockwaves fanning outward to the tips of my fingers and toes.

His hands rise until they can cup my breasts in his warm palms. "I've missed these so much."

"I've missed you touching me." No one has ever known my body the way he did.

"I want you to come for me, Vi."

Those eight little words make me shatter into a million pieces. The orgasm last night was amazing, but this...

Having him buried so deep inside my body that I don't know where I end and he begins is so much better.

As soon as I cry out, a groan tumbles from his lips. His hands drift from my breasts to my waist, biting into my flesh and holding me in place as he drives inside me.

That's all it takes for the years to fall away, along with the walls I'd carefully built around my heart to keep him out.

When the last shudder fades, I collapse on top of him. His arms slip around my ribcage to hold me against his chest.

"I love you, Vi. More than anything."

For the first time in three years, everything falls back into place, and it finally feels like I can breathe again. "I love you, too."

"No matter what happens," he says, staring deep into my eyes, "you'll always be my girl."

The End

Dare you to Love me

WESTERN WILDCATS novela

USA Today Bestselling Author
JENNIFER SUCEVIC

1

RIGGS

Stella drops her floral duffle in the corner of my room. "Are you sure you don't mind me staying for a few days?"

I roll my eyes.

Why is this girl even asking?

She has to know that whatever she needs, I'm here for her.

"Hell, no. I already told you—stay as long as you want. It's not a problem."

She tilts her blonde head just a bit before searching my face. "You don't mind sharing your room with me?" There's a slight pause as she shifts. "The last thing I want to do is get in your way. What happens if you want to bring a girl up here and...you know..." Her voice trails off.

It's steadily that I hold her gaze. "Trust me, you don't have to worry about that."

When she arches her brows as if encouraging me to explain, I clear my throat and steer the topic in a different direction.

It takes effort to lighten my tone. "If you're not comfortable sharing a bed, I can always bunk with one of the guys or on the couch downstairs."

Her face scrunches. "Eww. That's disgusting. I wouldn't make my worst enemy sleep on that couch."

It's no secret that the oversized piece of furniture in the living room has seen *way* too much action over the years. Some of which has probably been embedded in the fabric for all eternity.

"It'll be like when we used to have sleepovers," she says. "Remember?"

Of course I do. Stella and I have known each other since elementary school. Her house was situated in back of mine and it didn't take long for us to become thick as thieves. And nothing in all these years has altered that.

All right so maybe that's not a hundred percent true. It was sometime during freshman year of high school that my feelings for her began to change. They've slowly deepened, growing into something more.

Have I ever acted on them?

Hell, no.

Are you kidding me?

Stella doesn't see me as anything other than her bestie.

How do I know this?

Because she has absolutely no problem talking to me about all the dates she goes on.

FYI—that girl goes through guys the way some people go through underwear. I've had cartons of milk sitting in my fridge that have been around longer than some of her so-called boyfriends.

I force a smile before shoving those thoughts away. "Sure do. Don't worry, it'll be fun. Just like old times. Did I mention that the guys are throwing a party tonight? We can hang out and have a few drinks."

And I'll do my damnedest not to obsess about what it'll be like to have her all to myself in my bed.

A frown flickers across her expression. "You should have said something sooner. I already made plans for the evening."

Everything inside me nosedives as I attempt to keep my response casual. "Oh?"

With a shrug, she swings away, squatting to rifle through her duffle bag. "Yeah, someone I met on the Western U dating app."

I cross my arms against my chest and grit my teeth so tightly that it feels like the molars are in imminent danger of shattering. It takes a concerted effort to unlock my jaw. I fucking hate the idea of her going out with another dude.

Especially when she's coming home to me at the end of the night.

I straighten to my full height as another thought slams into me with the force of a two-by-four. "You're, ah, planning on sleeping here...right?"

If she doesn't, I'll—

She tosses a mischievous glance over her shoulder before flashing a sly grin. "I'll let you know if things go *really* well, and I spend the night elsewhere."

What?

Oh.

Hell.

No.

A tortured groan escapes from me at the idea of her having sex with someone else when her ass should be in my bed.

Her brow furrows as she sends another glance over her shoulder. "I'm sorry, did you say something?"

I clear my throat. "Just that you should bring him by afterward."

So I can pummel his ass.

With her clothes for the evening in hand, she pops back up before swallowing the distance between us and pressing a light kiss against my cheek.

"You're the absolute best, know that?"

Unfortunately for me, the *absolute best* apparently isn't what she's looking for.

Before I can suss out the situation any further, she disappears through the bedroom door and into the bathroom to change.

2

STELLA

The front porch of the hockey house is strung with colorful lights that blink in the darkness, giving the dilapidated old Victorian a festive appearance. There's a six-foot evergreen shoved in the corner. It's decorated with pucks and white hockey stick tape. Upon closer inspection, there are also metal beer caps with holes punched at the top and threaded with string that dangles from branches.

Even though the windows are closed to keep out the frigid air, music pours from the house. It could be heard from down the block where we parked. Riggs wasn't kidding when he said the guys were throwing a party. From the looks of it, half the university showed up to help celebrate how well the team is doing this season. Everyone's excited for them to make it to the Frozen Four and bring home another championship title.

Go Wildcats!

Ever since Riggs started playing hockey in first grade, I've been a diehard fan. I've only missed a handful of games over the years and love watching him on the ice. He looks larger than life on skates and with the shoulder pads. His dark hair, longer than usual, peeks out from the back of his helmet.

It's sexy.

As soon as a shiver dances down my spine, I shove those disturbing thoughts from my head and refocus my attention on my date. Nick keeps pace with me as I ground to a halt outside the front door. I'm more than ready to say goodnight.

This date has turned out to be a total bust.

I give it two out of five stars along with a solid *would not recommend*.

Only wanting to put an end to this evening, I mentioned several times on the way over that he didn't need to walk me to the door, but he insisted.

Nick nods toward the house as he shoves his hands into the pockets of his jeans. "So, you live here?"

"Nope. A pipe burst in my apartment this morning, so I'm staying with a friend for a couple days." My fingers wrap around the door handle as I pop it open a few inches. "I mentioned it earlier when you picked me up."

His gaze flickers my way before he cranes his neck to get a better look at the mayhem ensuing inside. "Oh, yeah. Right. Must have slipped my mind."

Or you just didn't care enough to pay attention.

Instead of inviting him inside, I force a smile. It took less than fifteen minutes in his company to realize it wasn't going to work out. The only thing we have in common is that we're both hockey fans. But there's zero attraction to speak of. He's the exact opposite of what I'm usually attracted to.

Full disclosure—this little experiment was intentional on my part.

Last month, I noticed that all the guys I normally go for all have a similar vibe. They're muscular athletes with dark, messy hair that's a tad too long. It wasn't until I took a step back and analyzed the situation that I realized they all resembled my bestie.

So, I decided to look for someone who was the complete opposite. Unfortunately, that backfired.

Now I just want to say goodbye and find Riggs. I'm sure he'll laugh his ass off when I admit how sucky tonight was. Although, I certainly won't be telling him the reason why.

I should probably get off these dating apps.

Clearly, they're not working.

"So, this was nice. Thanks for walking me to the door..." My voice trails off, hoping he'll get the hint that tonight is officially over. At least it is for us. Although, he hasn't picked up on any of the subtle clues I've been dropping like breadcrumbs so I'm not sure why I'm expecting something different now.

"Yeah, it was definitely a good time." Instead of meeting my gaze, he stares past me through the crack in the door before laying his palm against the thick wood and shoving it farther open. His eyes widen as he points. "Hey, isn't that Ryder McAdams?"

I glance inside the living room and find the blond defenseman. "Yeah, it is. Do you know him?"

His gaze flickers to mine for a second as he shakes his head. "No, but I'm a huge fan."

Of course you are.

A sigh escapes from me.

This is one of the reasons I don't advertise that I'm friends with Riggs Stranton. Or that my brother is Brody McKinnon. I got enough of that when I was growing up. People who only wanted to befriend me in order to get closer to them. I want to be liked for *me*. Not because my brother played in the NHL for more than a decade. Or my bestie has the possibility of turning pro in the not-so-distant future.

"Wait a minute...is this the hockey house? Is that where you're staying?" His voice escalates with every word.

"Yup, my friend is on the team," I reluctantly admit.

He perks up and nearly shouts, "Well, why didn't you say so? Now you can introduce me to all the guys. How could you forget to mention something so important?" He shakes his head.

"*What?*" Before I can tell him that wasn't in the cards tonight, Nick pushes past me. More music and voices drift out to the porch as I stare after him.

Irritated by the turn tonight has taken, I reluctantly step inside and close the front door. A dozen or so of the guys are wearing Santa hats and ugly sweaters. Colby McNichols has a red hat along with a big white beard, minus the festive sweater. He's lounging on a chair with a girl perched on his lap. She's stroking her hands over his bare chest. The guy looks like he was carved from marble.

That's not an exaggeration.

There's a line of girls waiting patiently for their turn on his lap as if he's actually Santa Clause.

It's tempting to shake my head.

Colby has to be one of the biggest flirts on this campus.

And the dimples...

My god the dimples.

My heart has actually melted when they've been flashed in my direction, and I'd like to think I'm made of sterner stuff.

My gaze skims over the sea of students before landing on Riggs. He's a little bit taller at six foot three than most of the people who surround him. A good number of them are girls vying for his attention. The moment our gazes fasten, a wide smile breaks out across his face before he lifts a hand to wave. Something unwanted warms my chest before spreading outward.

His gaze flickers to the guy I'm reluctantly trailing behind before he pops a brow. I roll my eyes and shake my head, silently pleading with him not to ask.

Nick's mouth falls open as he grounds to a halt. "Holy shit! Is that Riggs Stranton? I love that dude!"

Before I can respond, he practically shoves me out of his way and plows through the thick crowd until he reaches the dark-haired defenseman. I end up knocking into a girl just as she's about to take a drink from her red cup. Half of the golden liquid gets dumped down the front of the reindeer T-shirt that clings to her like a second skin.

My face heats as I mutter an apology and shimmy past her. When I glance at Riggs for a second time, he's grinning ear to ear and his broad shoulders are shaking with amusement.

With gritted teeth, I reluctantly trail after my date until I reach my bestie. He's already being bombarded with a flurry of questions.

Even after I arrive, Nick doesn't bother to acknowledge my presence.

Or apologize for pushing me out of the way.

What a jerk.

Riggs' steady gaze stays locked on mine as Nick continues to fangirl. Just in case you're wondering, second-hand embarrassment is a real thing. At this very moment, I'm being eaten alive by it. I can already tell by Riggs' smirk that I won't be hearing the end of this for a while.

When Nick launches into a game from a couple weeks ago where Riggs scored two goals in quick succession, I mutter, "I'm going to grab a drink." I need to get away from this guy before I totally lose it. With any luck, he'll be gone when I return.

Although, that's probably wishful thinking on my part. From the looks of him, he's in heaven. He might never leave the house.

In a shocking twist I didn't see coming, Nick finally glances my way. "That would be great. Could you grab one for me, too?"

My death stare has absolutely no effect on him.

With that, he dismisses me before pelting Riggs with more questions about the hockey team.

"Sure, no problem," I mutter, swinging away and heading for the kitchen where a makeshift bar is set up.

On the way, I pass by Juliette and pull her in for a quick hug. She's technically my niece, but we're more like cousins or even sisters since we're the same age and grew up together. Ryder, her boyfriend, has a brawny arm slung around her shoulders. Now that they're officially an item, he never lets her stray too far.

Carina, Juliette's roommate, is also here with her boyfriend, Ford. They're a newly minted couple who have been together for a handful of weeks. Others might be surprised that the ex-stepsiblings are now dating but not me. I had the sneaking suspicion by the way he'd tease her mercilessly that his feelings for her ran deep.

When Ford leans in to nip at her bottom lip, Carina nearly melts into a puddle of goo.

And who can blame her?

Ford Hamilton is hot with mahogany-colored hair, golden, honey-colored eyes, and muscles for miles.

As good looking as Ford is, he doesn't hold a candle to Riggs, who also has rich brown hair, although his is a little shaggier. He should have had a trim a couple weeks ago, but I like the length. His face is made up of sharp angles that hint at the Russian heritage on his mother's side. His body is just as chiseled from working out and skating six days a week.

Over the last decade, I've seen him grow from gangly boy into droolworthy man. As much as I don't want to notice, it would be impossible not to. And I'm certainly not the only one. I'm more than aware of how the girls on this campus clamor for his attention.

I certainly can't blame them for wanting to get closer to the hunky defenseman.

Even when it feels like I'm being eaten up with jealousy.

As soon as that sly thought pops into my brain, I shove it away before greeting a couple of the guys from the team. Wolf Westerville, Madden Caruso, Hayes Van Doren, and Bridger Sanderson. Bridger's got a black Western Wildcats hockey ballcap pulled low over his eyes. For the past month or so, unsavory texts have been popping up on the university message system that gets blasted out to both staff and students. Ever since then, he's been trying to keep a low profile.

Maverick, Juliette's brother, and my nephew, pulls me in for a hug. We've always been close too. He's more like a brother than anything else. Just like Ryder, he'll end up playing for the NHL after college. Especially with his father, Brody, carefully guiding his career.

After grabbing two bottles of beer from the fridge, I make my way back to the living room. It's tempting to ditch Nick, but how can I leave Riggs with that stage-five clinger?

My shoulders droop, because the answer is that I can't.

Just as I pass a short hallway that leads to the first-floor bathroom, strong fingers wrap around my bicep and tug me into the darkness.

My heart jolts at the unexpected contact as I'm hauled against a broad chest. In the shadowiness of the hall, I find myself staring up into Rigg's chocolate-colored depths. They're so dark in their intensity.

His gaze burns into mine as air gets clogged in my lungs.

This kind of unwanted reaction has been happening with more frequency.

Even worse than that—I have no idea how to make it stop.

I open my mouth to say something—*anything*—but not a single sound escapes.

"I couldn't take the questions anymore, so I ditched the guy."

The low notes of his voice scrape something deep inside my belly. It takes effort to shake off the fog that's trying to cocoon its way around me.

"Is that why you're here, lurking in the shadows?"

"Yup." He rips his gaze from mine long enough to scan the thick crowd of partiers. "Think there's any chance that he'll give up and go home?"

That question is enough to dissolve the confusing cocktail of emotions that flared to life at his close proximity. Even though I don't necessarily want to, I take a step in retreat so that we're no longer touching.

Only then does my heartbeat settle into a normal rhythm.

The last thing I want is to blur the lines of our friendship. We've been besties for way too many years to throw it away on a bit of sexual attraction. No matter how long I live, there will never be another friend like Riggs.

When his gaze resettles on mine and he continues to silently stare, I gesture toward the living room. "We should probably get back to the party."

His voice dips. "If that's what you want."

Heat pools in my core.

Maybe it's not what I want, but it's what I need.

3

RIGGS

From the corner of my eye, I notice Stella's date has cornered Garret Akeman, one of the senior guys on the team and is yapping his damn ear off. From the irritated expression on Akeman's face, he's not happy about it and is looking for a way to escape.

A smile twitches around the corners of my lips.

I get along with most of the guys on the team—we're more like brothers than anything else. Garret Akeman is the exception. Most of us can't stand the dude. He thinks he's god's gift to hockey.

Newsflash—he's not.

On top of that, he's an asshole.

I tow Stella through the crowded living area where most of the party has congregated before turning into a smaller room that has a big screen television. A couple guys are chilling out and playing video games while others are settled on the couch and chair.

"Riggs, get your ass over here. We're just about to play a game of truth or dare," Ford says, flashing a grin at Carina like it's some kind of inside joke.

I glance at Stella and raise my brows in silent askance. When she shrugs, we squeeze in next to Ryder and Juliette. Shocker—there's a girl perched on Colby's lap.

A couple of our younger teammates are also playing. Puck bunnies hover around the players, hoping to get chosen for a dare. I'm sure if you asked them to strip down and do the nasty in front of everyone, they'd oblige without question.

Thank fuck Stella's never been into any of my teammates. I'm sure that's because she grew up with a famous brother who played professionally. She's not impressed by these guys. Not even the ones who'll get picked up by the NHL.

A few more people trickle into the room and join the game. I notice a couple of the younger guys checking Stella out. I can't blame them. She's gorgeous with bright blue eyes, long blonde hair, and an hourglass figure. That being said, I shoot them dark looks before throwing my arm around her shoulders and hauling her close.

Damn but she feels good tucked against my body.

When she glances at me, I flash a tight smile. My muscles loosen when she makes no attempt to shrug off my hold. We've always been affectionate with each other. But for some reason, something feels off tonight. There's an electricity that crackles in the air like an impending storm. The confusion that flickers in her eyes tells me that she's just as aware of it as I am.

"Truth or dare, Stella."

She rips her gaze from me to glance at Colby.

Almost immediately, I feel the loss of it.

"Dare."

I tense, afraid that he'll goad her into doing something with another guy. If that happens, I'll take him out during our next practice.

See if I don't.

"I dare you to lock lips with our boy, Riggs."

Even though the music is blaring from the other room and the babble of voices surrounds us, I'm so attuned to the girl next to me that I hear the slight intake of her breath. My heart drops before slamming into overdrive. It takes effort to keep my face carefully blank so it doesn't give away the churn of my private thoughts.

Her movements freeze before she turns her head just enough to meet my eyes.

We've held hands and hugged plenty of times. The one thing we've never done is kiss.

It's a line I've never dared to cross.

Have I wanted to?

Fuck, yeah. A million times. But I've been too chickenshit to do it. Now that the opportunity has presented itself, I'll be damned if I don't take full advantage of it.

When Stella remains silent, Colby's grin grows wider. "Well, what's it gonna be, McKinnon? Taking the dare or drinking a shot?"

Her tongue darts out to moisten her lips. "I'll take the dare."

I can practically feel the blood that rushes through my veins as she swivels toward me. Even though questions don't fall from her lips, they lurk in her gorgeous depths. I nod to let her know that I'm down with this.

The knowledge that I might never get this chance again pounds through my head. It's what has me wrapping my hands around her waist and hauling her onto my lap so that she has to straddle my thighs. Her wide eyes stay pinned to mine as her hands drift to my shoulders. Only then do mine lift to cradle her cheeks.

Even though everyone in the room is focused on us, I block them out.

It's just her.

And me.

My attention stays locked on Stella as I draw her close enough for my lips to ghost over hers.

Once.

Twice.

On the third pass, my mouth settles over her plump flesh. My tongue sweeps across the seam of her lips, begging for entrance. When she doesn't immediately open, I tilt her head just a bit and come at her from a different angle. When she inhales a breath, I delve inside so our tongues can dance.

The movement is languid.

Erotic.

As if we have all the time in the world and my teammates and our friends aren't watching our first kiss unfold. Her sweetness explodes on my tongue. It's so damn tempting to crush her against my chest, but I've spent years listening to her talk about the guys she's dated. As much as it killed me to hear it, I've taken a shit ton of mental notes.

I know *exactly* what this girl likes.

How she wants to be touched.

What she craves in a partner.

What turns her on and what she doesn't like.

When she presses closer, becoming more of an active participant in the caress, everything around us fades to the background. I want to eat this girl alive. A groan rumbles up from my chest as my tongue slides against hers. Slow sweeps that have my cock stiffening in my joggers. There's no way she doesn't feel the thick length with the way she's pressed against me.

The game is long forgotten as my lips rove hungrily over hers.

I'm so wrapped up in her that I barely hear the asshole who clears their throat, breaking the delicate spell woven around us. My heart slams against my ribcage as if trying to break loose from the confines.

Stella jerks away with a small gasp. Her breath comes out in short, sharp pants as she searches my eyes as if seeing me for the first time. The dazed look that fills hers drives me fucking wild.

Know what I like even more?

That I'm the one who put it there.

Me.

"Ummm...wow. I think I just orgasmed," Carina murmurs.

"The hell you did, pretty girl," Ford says. "You're loud AF when you come."

She whacks him in the chest as a smile twitches around her lips.

"He's right, you totally are," Juliette adds with a laugh.

Color stains Carina's cheeks as she turns her attention to Ryder and jerks a brow. "I suppose you have something to add to the convo?"

Ryder smirks and pulls his girlfriend closer before pressing a kiss to her cheek. "I'm not saying a word. The only person's orgasms I'm concerned about are hers."

A few puck bunnies sigh.

"And that would be my cue to leave," Maverick McKinnon, Juliette's brother, grumbles as he stalks from the room.

I block out the conversation that swirls around me as my tongue darts out to swipe my lips. I've spent years contemplating what Stella would taste like. What I've just discovered is that reality is way better than I imagined.

The other thing I figured out?

One taste will never be enough to satiate the deep well of need that lives inside me where this girl is concerned.

4

STELLA

Hours later and I'm *still* thinking about that kiss. Even though neither of us has mentioned it, it's like an elephant sitting between us.

Or maybe it's just me.

Maybe I'm the only one dwelling on it.

When I stifle a yawn, Riggs leans closer, his warm breath stirring the hair near my ear. "Ready for bed? It's after midnight."

The low scrape of his voice has my belly doing a strange little flip flop.

Or maybe it's the question itself.

Although, it shouldn't. The two of us sharing a bed isn't new or a big deal. We've done it plenty of times before.

And yet...

It feels like a *huge* deal.

And I don't want it to.

I don't want anything to change between us.

Once you sleep with someone, the dynamics in your relationship shift. There's no way to stop it from happening. It's inevitable.

As much as I'd like to pretend otherwise, our connection has morphed into something new. Something different. It's like one day I suddenly noticed the way his joggers were slung low on his lean hips or how a chunk of his hair hung in his eyes. Whenever those little sparks of attraction flared to life, I've been diligent about stomping them out and pretending they never happened. For the most part, it hasn't been a problem.

Unfortunately, that kiss has blown my carefully constructed façade to smithereens, and I have no idea how to put the pieces back together again.

Or if it's even possible at this point.

Every time he says something, my gaze roves over his face, taking in all the subtle changes adulthood has wrought, before dipping to his mouth. The way his tongue will peek through his lips makes my panties flood with undeniable heat.

Someone needs to explain how one tiny kiss has rocked the very foundation of our friendship.

It doesn't make sense.

"Stell?"

I blink out of those thoughts and refocus my attention on Riggs. His head is cocked and he's staring at me with a heavy-lidded look. It's almost as if he knows exactly what's circling through my head.

Heat stings my cheeks.

How embarrassing would *that* be?

That kiss probably meant absolutely nothing to him and here I am, obsessing about it like a loser, because when it comes down to it…I can't remember the last time I locked lips with someone and it blew my world apart.

Have I ever been knocked off balance like that?

I almost wince, privately acknowledging the harsh truth to myself.

The only consolation I have is that there's been a long string of lousy dates in my not-so-distant past. Including the one tonight. That has to be the reason all these weird feelings have been roused, right?

It's embarrassing to realize that I have to redirect my thoughts for a second time. "Yeah?"

"I asked if you're ready to hit the sheets." A smirk curls around the edges of his lips.

For some reason, that question makes me feel even more tense. Like a tightly wound spring just waiting to go off.

As difficult as it is, I tear my gaze away from his and glance around the living room. With the late hour, the crowd has thinned. Maybe the best course of action would be to crash at Juliette's apartment. A little time and distance from Riggs would probably be enough to set everything to rights again.

Except…

Neither she nor Carina are anywhere to be found. When did they take off? And how didn't I notice?

Ugh. I'm stuck here. Guilt suffuses me because I don't mean it that way. Under normal circumstances, I love spending time with Riggs. But right now, it feels like we're in this really weird place and it's exactly where I don't want to be.

Left without any other recourse, I say, "Yup. I'm super tired. I'm sure I'll be out as soon as my head hits the pillow." At least, that's my hope. I just want to put tonight firmly behind us.

As soon as the words leave my lips, he pops to his feet and pulls me up. Before I realize it, he's dragging me through the crowd to the staircase and then up to the second floor. A handful of moments later, we're in his room. I stare at the queen-sized bed that dominates the space. I'm always popping over and hanging out, and this is the first time I've been hyperaware of it.

My hands tremble as I beeline for my duffle and rifle through it. Once my fingers lock around the soft cotton of my tank top, I hightail it to the safety of the bathroom. As soon as I slip inside and close the door, I lean against it and squeeze my eyelids tightly closed.

I really need to get a hold of myself. I'm acting like a twenty-one-year-old virgin who's never been within five feet of a boy before, and that's not who I am.

I need to stop dwelling on that kiss.

It didn't mean anything.

We were playing a stupid game.

It takes a full five minutes to wrangle my emotions back under control. By then, I realize I was right—all I needed was a bit of distance. The entire night, Riggs had his arm slung around my shoulders. The beachy scent of his cologne had slyly tangled around me, inundating my senses until I'd wanted to inhale a big breath of him.

It had just been too much.

It's almost laughable how wound up I got about it.

Ridiculous, even.

I'm sure in the morning, we'll both have a good chuckle.

That's what friends do, right?

Exactly.

It's only when I step back inside the room and catch sight of Riggs wearing nothing more than form-fitting, black boxer briefs that the tangle of my emotions crashes over me like a tidal wave, and I realize I'm in big trouble.

There's absolutely no way I'm going to forget about that lip lock or the sun-kissed flesh now on display.

Holy crap.

When the hell did Riggs get so muscly?

From where I'm standing, even his muscles have muscles.

Does this guy spend every waking minute in the gym?

As much as I should avert my eyes, I can't stop the way my hungry gaze licks over every delectable inch.

Neither of us moves or says a word. It's only when his gaze dips to my chest that I realize my nips are standing at attention. It's like a bolt of electricity sliding through me, sparking every cell to life. That's all the impetus I need to get my ass in gear and dive headfirst onto the bed before scampering beneath the covers. When I've drawn them up to my chin, I chance another peek at him.

God, I'm acting like such a ninny.

My heartbeat hitches when Riggs walks around to my side of the bed and stops to stare down at me. It would be impossible not to notice that I'm eye level with his package.

And it's...*bigger* than I imagined.

Not that I've, you know, thought about his package.

Much.

Argh.

This is bad.

"Do you need anything before I turn out the light?"

I shake my head. I'm much too afraid to open my mouth. I'm terrified that my voice will be nothing more than an unintelligible squeak that will give me away.

Look away from his dick, you little perv.

This is your bestie.

But I can't. It's like a horrific traffic accident.

My core contracts as another burst of heat floods my panties.

It's tempting to reach out and run my fingers over him. I tighten them until the rounded nails bite into my palms so I don't do exactly that.

Can you even imagine what would happen if I touched him?

I'd never be able to look my bestie in the eyes again.

A strange concoction of relief and disappointment spirals through me when he swings away. My gaze stays glued to his ass.

Hot damn, he has a nice backside.

A handful of seconds later the light is clicked off, plunging the room into blessed darkness, and he's sliding beneath the sheets. I close my eyes and will myself to fall into a deep, dreamless sleep. With any luck, I'll feel more like myself in the morning, and I can put all this nonsense behind me.

Behind us.

We can get back to normal.

"Stell?"

My eyes pop open as I stare up at the ceiling rather than at him. "Yeah?"

"You're not going to see that bozo again, are you?"

I snort out a laugh. It's enough to break the sexual tension, which is a welcome relief.

"No. I've already deleted him. In fact, I'll be deleting the app altogether."

"Good. You deserve way better." His tone dips. "I hope you realize that."

My heart softens as I roll toward him. I'm just able to make out his handsome features in the darkness. It's only then that I realize his eyes are already locked on me.

"Thanks."

He scoots closer until I'm able to feel the heat of his practically naked body. Air gets wedged at the back of my throat as he balances on his elbow and hovers over me.

His steady gaze sifts through mine in the darkness. "I'm serious, Stella. You deserve a man who's going to make you his first priority."

My heartbeat stutters.

Almost as if in slow motion, his face looms closer until his lips can drift over mine. Unlike earlier, I open immediately so that the velvety softness of his tongue can invade my mouth.

There's nothing rushed or frenzied about how the caress unfolds. I don't realize until the heat of his skin nearly singes my palms that they've settled against his chest. The hard slabs of muscle tighten beneath my fingers. It's so tempting to let them wander.

The kiss seems to stretch forever. He angles his head one way and then another. That's all it takes for me to lose track of both time and space. When Riggs finally pulls away, I realize we're both breathing hard.

That's the moment reality crashes over me. It's like a bucket of frigid water dumped over my head. I mutter a quick goodnight before rolling away onto my side. My muscles fill with tension as I silently wonder where our friendship goes from here.

Maybe I should broach the subject...

I don't know.

I don't know anything anymore.

It feels like our entire relationship is careening out of control.

It's almost a relief when his breathing turns deep and even.

That kiss...

I clench my thighs together, attempting to stymie the arousal that has once again flared to life deep in my core.

The only thing I know for certain is that tonight is going to be a long night.

5

RIGGS

I'm not sure what rouses me from a deep sleep.
A noise?
A shift of the mattress?
My eyelids flutter open as I attempt to find my bearings.

For a handful of seconds, I lie perfectly still and listen to the sounds that fill the room. My ears strain in the darkness, but there's nothing. Maybe it was my imagination all along.

Just as I'm about to drift off again, there's another faint noise.

A whimper.

One that sounds suspiciously like—

That's when everything from earlier slams into me and I remember that Stella is spending the night in my bed.

My muscles freeze.

Is she having a dream?

Or worse, a nightmare?

Another noise—one that's more guttural in nature—fills the air. The deep vibration of it goes straight to my dick. I've been with enough chicks to know what that sound means.

It's cautiously that I turn my head enough for my gaze to fall on the other side of the mattress. Air gets trapped in my lungs as Stella comes into view. Her back is slightly arched, and her chin is tipped upward, revealing the long line of her throat. Her knees are slightly raised beneath the covers.

It takes a second to realize that she's getting herself off.

Holy fuck.

And just like that, my cock becomes unbearably hard. A tortured groan rises in my chest. It takes every ounce of self-control to tamp it back down so it doesn't escape from my lips.

Now that my eyes have adjusted to the velvety darkness, I'm able to see the way her teeth sink into her plush lower lip. My tongue swipes across my own. I'm still able to taste her there. It's so damn tempting to close the space between us and trail my lips over the column of her throat.

To find the pulse point that thrums beneath her delicate flesh.

My gaze drops to her spread thighs. I'd give just about anything to see what she's doing beneath the blanket. The way she's stroking her soft little pussy, giving herself pleasure.

I don't realize that I've reached over and tugged on the comforter until her movements freeze and her head snaps in my direction, wide eyes locking on mine.

"Don't stop," I rasp, silently cursing myself.

I'll fucking die if she stops.

When she remains perfectly still, the expression on her face conflicted, I plead, *"Please. I want to watch you."*

She drags a shaky breath into her lungs before squeezing her eyelids tightly closed. When she widens her thighs, I carefully pull the blanket away until she's completely bared to my sight. Every movement is cautiously made. As if she's a wild animal who could bolt at any second.

It's only when my eyes lick over her body that I realize her tank top has been shoved up against her collarbone so that her breasts are on display. Her nipples have tightened into hard little peaks that beg to be sucked and played with. My hungry gaze drifts along her ribcage before sliding over the gentle curve of her belly and then dipping to her spread thighs.

I don't think I've ever seen anything as beautiful as Stella spread out completely naked as her fingers rub gentle circles around her clit before dipping to her entrance.

I might have been hard at the idea of her masturbating, but it's nothing compared to the raging boner I now have.

I inch closer, wanting to get a better look in the velvety darkness that blankets us. It's so damn tempting to reach out and run my fingers over her, but I'm afraid of pushing for too much. I need to content myself with simply watching. I sit up, wanting a better view. As I hover over her body, attempting to see every inch, her eyelids flutter open and her gaze locks on mine.

"You're so fucking beautiful, you know that?"

Those soft words have her legs falling open even farther, giving me a tantalizing view of heaven. My dick throbs painfully in my boxer briefs as she continues stroking herself. I'd give my left nut just to slide inside the heat of her body and feel her muscles clench around me, milking every last drop of cum.

Fuck.

I want this moment to last forever.

Breathy little moans fall from her lips as she works her flesh. There's a part of me that can't believe she's allowing me to watch something I've spent all these years secretly fantasizing about.

When she finally shatters, it takes every ounce of control not to come in my boxers. A handful of seconds later, her muscles turn lax and a contented breath escapes from her. I don't realize that I've wrapped my fingers around her smaller ones until she glances at me, eyes full of questions.

My gaze stays pinned to hers as I lift them to my lips before sucking them deep inside my mouth. It's only when I've licked them clean and the honeyed taste of her floods my senses that I release her fingers and flop onto my back with a groan before throwing an arm over my eyes.

"Feel better?" I ask. My voice sounds scraped raw. Even to my own ears.

An embarrassed laugh escapes from her. "Yeah. You?"

If that's a joke, it's not funny.

"Hell no. I'm hard as fuck. I have no idea how I'm going to fall asleep after *that*."

One silent heartbeat passes.

Then another.

"Why don't you take care of yourself?"

I lift my arm and twist my head to stare at her as my brows skyrocket. "Are you serious?"

She shrugs. "Why not? Then maybe I won't feel like such a deviant."

It's so damn tempting to take her up on that offer.

I study her carefully in the darkness. "Are you sure?"

This feels like uncharted territory between us.

Have I dreamed about it?

Fuck, yeah.

And I've whacked off to thoughts of it.

But still…

We've always been such close friends. It would fucking kill me if Stella distanced herself because we crossed a line. I'd much rather we remain platonic than have nothing at all.

"Yeah." I silently mourn the loss of her breasts when she tugs the tank down before curling onto her side and staring at me with heavy-lidded eyes. "I want to watch you."

Fuck.

How am I supposed to turn down just such a request?

The answer is simple—I can't.

6

STELLA

As soon as I give him the green light to proceed, Riggs strips off his boxers. Had he just shoved them down and freed his erection, I would have been secretly disappointed. Now I get to see all of him.

Every delicious inch.

My greedy gaze takes in the dark hair that whirls across his chest before arrowing down his chiseled abdominals and then further to his groin. His hard cock stands proudly to attention as it curves toward his six pack. His thighs are thick and muscular from skating six days a week.

And he thinks I'm the beautiful one?

Ha!

The guy is delusional. It's him.

His gaze captures mine as he sucks the corner of his lip into his mouth and chews it as if silently contemplating something before his hand drifts to his dick and tightens around the girth.

My mouth turns cottony as I eat him up with my eyes.

When he clears his throat, my gaze flickers upward.

"What's wrong?"

"Can I..." His husky voice trails off.

"Can you what?"

"Can I rub my dick against you?"

My pussy clenches at the idea of such intimacy.

"Sure," I whisper, aroused beyond belief by the thought.

He quickly rolls to his side and pops to his knees before lifting one of my legs and positioning himself between them. My heartbeat explodes in my chest as his gaze clings to mine. With his fingers wrapped around my knees, he widens them, making room before moving closer until his thick cock is nestled against my center.

A groan escapes from him as he flexes his hips and runs his erection across my slit. He continues to move closer until I can feel every inch of his length pressed against me. My back arches at the delicious contact.

A shiver slides through me at the sight of a naked Riggs looming between my spread thighs. I've seen him in board shorts at the beach and in his boxers, but never like this. Every muscle is taut and straining as his thick cock juts toward me.

The sight of him is so damn sexy.

"Take off your tank," he growls. "I want to see your breasts again. They're so fucking perfect. All of you is."

It never occurs to me to turn down the request. My fingers tighten around the hem before dragging it up my torso and over my head.

And then I'm as naked as he is.

He pushes my thighs farther apart and flexes his hips. Every time the mushroom-shaped head bumps my clit, toe-curling sensation ricochets through my body and I realize it won't take much to orgasm for a second time.

Especially with the way he's stroking his hard length against me. I can't help but squirm, wanting more.

What would it feel like to have his thick erection buried deep inside me?

Filling me to the brim.

Needing more sensation, my hands rise to my breasts, squeezing the softness before trailing the fingertips over my nipples. With my gaze locked on him, I tweak the tips until they're so hard, they ache.

"Fuck, Stella…"

One more thrust of his hips and he's coming undone. His dick strokes my clit as his hot release lands on my lower belly. He arches his back and bares his throat as a groan rumbles up from deep within his chest. The low tones of it reverberate throughout my entire being. That's all it takes for me to tumble over the edge. As I grind my pussy against his steely length, stars burst behind my eyelids.

As intense as the first orgasm was, this is even more so.

When I finally float back to earth, I find Riggs staring down at the ejaculation painted across my lower abdomen. My thighs are still spread impossibly wide with his cock nestled against me. Even though he just came, he's still hard.

My gaze stays locked on his as I run my fingers through his release before lifting them to my mouth and taking a long lap.

His eyes widen.

"Now we're even."

"*Oh fuck.*"

7

RIGGS

I wake with a lazy stretch. My eyes aren't even cracked open yet, and already there's a smile etched across my lips.

Have I ever woken up and felt this amazing?

Like I could conquer the fucking world single handedly?

Nope, don't think—

That's when everything from the night before crashes back to me.

We might not have had sex, but it was the single hottest experience of my life.

And it happened with Stella!

Somehow, I just knew it would be like this between us.

We've always been best friends and the sexual chemistry we were able to generate was off the charts. Is there a reason we can't turn this into something long term?

Something permanent?

We both had a good time. Adding a physical aspect to our relationship will only strengthen it.

Decision made, I roll over, more than ready for a repeat performance.

Except...

The bed is empty.

I slide my hand over the sheets. The cotton is cool to the touch. It's almost enough to make me wonder if I dreamed the entire episode.

Is it possible she slipped away to use the bathroom?

I sit up and glance around the room, searching for clues to her whereabouts. My gaze settles on the corner where she'd dropped her duffle yesterday afternoon only to find it missing.

That's all it takes for the good vibes humming beneath my skin to vanish into thin air. I swear under my breath before whipping off the covers and rolling from the bed. My mind cartwheels as I stalk to the dresser and grab joggers and a T-shirt, along with a sweatshirt before rushing through the door and down the staircase.

I find Hayes in the kitchen, leaning against the counter. His messy, golden-brown hair is all over the place as he dips his spoon into a massive bowl before shoving cereal into his mouth.

"Sup," he says with a chin lift.

I don't bother with pleasantries. "Have you seen Stella?"

He continues to chew all the while eyeing me up. "Yeah. She lit out of here like her ass was on fire about thirty minutes ago."

I drag a hand through my hair and pull the cell from my pocket before hitting her number. A second or two later it goes straight to voicemail. A scowl morphs across my face.

Is she seriously going to ignore my call?

That's a fucking first.

Left without any other recourse, I fire off a text and wait impatiently for a response.

Sixty seconds slowly tick by.

Then another minute passes.

By the third one, it becomes glaringly apparent that she has zero intention of responding. What scares me more than anything is that I might have fucked up our friendship.

It's tempting to go out and look for her, but I can't. We have practice in less than an hour.

Maybe the best thing I can do is give her a little bit of space to clear her head.

But that's all she gets.
Then, whether she likes it or not, I'm coming for her.
Stella can run, but she can't hide.
Not from me.
Not from *us*.

8

STELLA

I lift the candy cane mocha with extra whipped cream to my mouth and take a drink. It's filled with pepperminty goodness. Each small sip helps settle my nerves.

I'm tucked into a corner at the Roasted Bean coffee shop on campus. The place is fully decked out for Christmas with a seven-foot-tall tree parked beside the register, twinkling stars that dance in the windows, evergreen garland draped across the top and dangling down the sides of the chalkboard menu, along with glass ornaments filled with coffee beans that hang from the ceiling above the counter. As if that wasn't enough holiday overload, all of the employees are wearing headbands with adorable reindeer antlers.

It's like Christmas threw up all over the place.

And I absolutely love it.

This is one of my favorite times of year.

Hockey season being a close second. That thought only turns my attention back to Riggs.

Ugh.

I don't know what to do.

He's fired off a dozen texts and tried calling an equal number of times.

I feel like the world's biggest coward for sneaking out the way I did this morning.

It's not who I am.

But...

In the harsh light of dawn, everything that happened the night before feels like too much. Like we crossed a line that we'll never be able to come back from. What I'm most scared of is that we've set fire to our relationship.

How is it possible to go back to being just friends after an experience like that?

Maybe we didn't have sex, but it had come damn close. His thick length had rubbed against me in the most intimate way, making me a hot and needy mess. I've never experienced anything like it before.

How am I supposed to pretend it never happened?

Is that even possible?

And it all started because the guy caught me masturbating.

While sleeping next to him.

Heat scalds my cheeks at the memory.

Instead of plowing my way through homework, which had been my intention when I'd set up camp on the couch in the coffee shop, I can't stop dwelling on last night.

A mortified groan works its way up my throat.

What I've come to realize is that as much as I've been trying to keep everything platonic with Riggs, it hasn't been that way for a while. The feelings that reared their ugly head yesterday aren't new.

Although, acknowledging their presence is.

Unable to help myself, I pull out my phone and take another peek at the slew of messages.

He wants to know where I am.

I've yet to respond.

What we both need is a breather before finally sitting down and hashing this out. With any luck, we'll be able to course correct and everything will go back to the way it was.

That's what I want, right?

If my heart clenches at the idea, I quickly brush it aside and ignore it.

My finger hovers over the miniature keyboard before ultimately deciding against opening up the lines of communication. Once I do that, there's no going back. It's carefully that I set the slim device on the coffee table next to my drink.

I'll text him later.

He'll see that I'm doing what's best for both of us.

I pick up my textbook and attempt to focus on what I'm reading. It's only when I reach the bottom of the section that I realize I haven't absorbed a single concept. A huff of annoyance escapes from me as I resign myself to reading the page for what feels like the millionth time. Barely do I make it through the first sentence when someone drops down beside me.

My eyes widen as they land on Riggs.

His hair is all damp and shiny and I realize that he probably just came from practice.

One glance at his expression tells me that he's angry.

I've seen him look at other people like that but never me.

Moisture springs to my palms as a sick knot twists in the pit of my belly.

In all honesty, I can't remember the last time we had a simple disagreement.

Before I can open my mouth or wrap my brain around what I want to say, he snaps, "We need to talk."

I straighten my shoulders and jerk my head into a stiff nod, knowing that I can't put off this conversation any longer.

"We should go out," he says.

"We should take a break," I blurt at the same time.

A second of silence ticks by as we both frown, digesting what the other person said.

"What? You want to take a break?" His eyes widen as his hand flies to his chest. "*From me?*"

The way his voice escalates with each word leaves me wincing.

Never in my wildest dreams could I have imagined a convo like this with Riggs. We've been friends for so long that I can barely remember a time in my life when he wasn't filling it. And I certainly can't imagine what it would be like to move forward without him by my side. Sure, I'd still have Juliette, but it wouldn't be the same. Riggs is a massive presence in my life.

Without him...

Even the idea makes my heart throb a painful beat beneath my breast. It's tempting to lift my hand and rub the spot.

I clear my throat and shift on the cushion. "Don't you think it would be best for our friendship if we took a step back? Just for a little bit?"

He draws in a deep breath before forcing it out again, almost as if trying to center himself. The tension filling his muscles loosens as he pries the textbook from my hands and sets it carefully on the coffee table before threading our fingers together.

My gaze drops to them.

"Why should we do that?" he asks calmly.

My eyes lift to his. "Because of what happened last night."

He strains closer before dropping his voice. His gaze never falters from my own. If anything, it only intensifies. It feels as if I've been caught within the crosshairs of it.

"Last night was the single hottest night of my life, and the fact that it was with you makes it even better. I love you, Stella. I've *always* loved you."

"As a friend," I murmur. "You love me as a *friend*."

It's slowly that he shakes his head. "I love you as more than that. I have for a while." He jerks his shoulders before admitting, "I just wasn't sure if you could ever feel the same about me."

He's felt this way for a while?

How didn't I realize it?

"But our friendship...I don't want to lose it."

He swallows up the small bit of space between us until I'm able to see all the chocolaty-colored flecks that make up his irises as his warm breath drifts across my lips.

"I promise that will never happen. No matter what, we'll always be friends. But I want more, Stella. I want to be the man in your life. I want to hold you in my arms at night." His voice turns rough, sounding as if it's been scraped raw. "More than that, I want to be your everything, just like you're mine."

Tears prick the backs of my eyes as I reveal what's in my heart. "You already are my everything."

His gaze searches mine, sifting through all my private thoughts. "Do you trust me?"

"Of course I do."

"Then let's give this a shot. *A real shot.* I promise, baby, you won't regret it. I'd move both heaven and hell to make you happy."

My teeth scrape across my lip as I watch the emotion swirl through his eyes. It feels a little bit like I'm leaping off a cliff into the abyss. It's terrifying. I have no idea if I'll land safely or not. But I trust Riggs.

I force out a slow, shaky breath. "Okay."

He tugs me onto his lap before nipping my bottom lip with sharp teeth. And just like yesterday, arousal shoots through me, lighting me up from the inside out.

That's all it takes for his eyes to darken with pent-up desire. "I haven't been able to stop thinking about last night."

Heat pools in my core as I admit, "Me neither."

Barely does my response escape before his lips descend, settling over mine. His tongue sweeps over the seam and without further prodding, I open so they can tangle. Shivers dance down my spine as electricity hums in the charged air.

A whimper of need breaks free from me.

"Hey, get a room," someone yells.

Riggs pulls away just enough to growl as he stares into my eyes, "I think that's an excellent idea."

His hands wrap around my waist, lifting me to my feet as he pops to his. Then he shoves my books into my bag and throws the strap over his shoulder.

"You ready to get out of here?"

A smile lifts the corners of my lips as I nod. "Yeah, I am."

With that, he tugs my fingers, towing me from the coffee shop and into the chilled morning air.

9

RIGGS

Unable to hold off for another moment, my lips crash onto hers as we make our way up the concrete walkway that cuts through a swath of snow-covered lawn to the house I share with my teammates.

Now that I've finally gotten a taste of Stella, I have no idea how I went so long without it. She's like the very air needed for survival.

And so damn sweet.

Once we make it up the rickety front porch stairs, my hand scrabbles for the handle without lifting my mouth from hers. My fingers wrap around cold metal before shoving open the door and steering us carefully over the threshold and into the entryway.

I'm well aware that this would go a lot faster if I'd just take a step in retreat, but I can't bring myself to do it. Driving over here from campus without mauling her was a feat in itself. I broke about ten different traffic laws in my rush to get home. Her hand was firmly ensconced in mine the entire time. Barely could I drag my gaze away. I was afraid that if I did, she'd vanish into thin air.

Or worse, I'd wake up and realize this had been nothing more than a dream.

I've wanted Stella for far too long, and now that I actually have her, I refuse to let go.

"See? Told you something was going on between them. That kiss last night was too damn hot to be just friends. You owe me twenty." I break away long enough to glare at Hayes. A grin slides across his face as he pops his shoulders in a careless shrug. "What? I saw this coming from a mile away." He elbows Bridger before rolling his eyes. "Not like this guy."

My other teammate glares. "Thanks a lot. Now I owe this dumbass money."

Instead of responding, I scoop Stella into my arms and carry her up the staircase to the second floor. The warm weight of her against me feels so damn good.

She buries her face against my chest. "I'm so embarrassed."

A chuckle escapes from me. "Why? Because everyone around us could see that I was in love with you? Except for, you know, *you*."

She lifts her face until her eyes can fasten onto mine. "I'm sorry, Riggs."

"Don't be. Our relationship is right where it's supposed to be. Don't ever doubt it."

I press my lips to hers before crossing the threshold of my room and closing the door. Then I twist the lock for good measure. I don't want any interruptions. If my roommates are smart, they won't even think about disturbing us until tomorrow. Maybe the day after that. Because now that I finally have Stella exactly where I want her—in my bed—it'll be a long damn time before I allow her to leave it.

Even though I'm reluctant to relinquish my hold, I set her on the queen-sized mattress before straightening to my full height. My fingers grip the hem of my sweatshirt, peeling it off along with the T-shirt. Her pupils dilate, the black swallowing up the blue, as her gaze roves over my bare chest. I can't help but stand perfectly still, allowing her to drink in the sight of me as sunlight pours in through the windows. If I questioned for even a second that she might not be attracted to me, the way she eats me up with her eyes only reconfirms that she feels the same way as I do.

Her attention dips to the thick jut of my erection covered by the joggers. Already, I'm hard as steel.

Her tongue darts out to moisten her lips as she shifts on the bed. "Aren't you going to take off the rest?"

A slow smile tugs at the corners of my lips. "Just waiting for you to give me the word."

"Word."

I snort and shove the cotton material down my legs before kicking them off so that I'm completely naked. Her gaze resettles on my cock. I can almost feel the heat of her perusal as it slowly licks over me.

Nothing has ever felt better.

"You're so beautiful," she murmurs.

I shake my head. "No, baby. You're the beautiful one."

With that, I swallow up the distance between us, crawling onto the mattress and up her body until she's lying flat.

There's so much trust swimming around within her blue depths as they cling to mine.

The one thing I'll never do is break it.

I nip her lower lip and suck the plump flesh into my mouth. After a handful of seconds, I release it with a gentle pop before peppering her face with soft kisses. It's only when I've adored every inch that I slide down the slender column of her throat and bathe the fluttering pulse with my tongue.

When I reach the collar of her sweater, I sit up and wrestle the wool up her torso before pulling it over her head and discarding it. The pink, cotton candy colored bra is the next item to get removed. I sit back so that my gaze can stroke over her lush curves.

She's even more perfect in the undiluted sunlight that streams in through the window. My palms settle over her breasts, squeezing the soft flesh. When she'd touched herself last night, it had taken every ounce of control not to go off like a shot.

It reminds me of summer and how we'd hang out at the swimming pool or the beach. I'd salivate over the tiny bikinis she'd wear, wanting to rip them off her body. I knew she'd be more than a handful.

And I wasn't wrong. Her breasts are generous in size with dark pink stained nipples. I can't help but tweak them, watching as they stiffen right up.

"How are you this perfect?"

Instead of responding, her fingers wrap around my cock before she slowly runs her palm over the thick length. I can't help but arch into her touch, needing more.

Needing everything she's willing to give.

I don't realize that I've closed the space between us until her pouty lips wrap around the head of my dick before she sucks me into her mouth.

Fuck.

I don't think anything has ever felt so amazing. Her gaze stays locked on mine as her cheeks hollow and she takes me so deep that I nudge the back of her throat.

A sharp hiss escapes from me. "That feels so damn good."

As loathe as I am to pull out, there's no way I'll be able to stop myself from coming if she keeps this up.

"Stella...you need to stop."

She smirks around my girth as a teasing glint enters her eyes and her mouth turns voracious.

"When I come again, it'll be inside your pussy," I growl before pulling away. "Not that pretty little mouth."

A second later, my cock pops free.

Arousal floods my system as I lean down and kiss her. "You just wait until I get my lips on you. Two can play at this game."

A delicate shiver slides through her. "Looking forward to it."

Me, too.

I've always enjoyed sex. But not like this. Before, it was just a way to get my rocks off or relieve stress. This...

Is so much more.

And it means absolutely everything.

I lick my way down her throat and collarbone until reaching her breasts. My tongue circles one pert tip before sucking it deep into my mouth. It doesn't take long for her spine to arch. I release the first one before giving the same attention to the other side. I've spent years dreaming about her breasts and wanting to play with them. Turns out reality is even better than what I imagined. I could spend hours sucking on her while palming the softness.

And if I have my way, that's exactly what will happen.

I want to worship every delectable inch of this girl.

It's only when she's writhing beneath me that I sink farther down her body before reaching the waistband of her leggings.

As my fingers slide beneath the elastic band, I glance up. "I want you to be sure about this. No regrets."

I don't think I could bear for that to happen.

I was beside myself when I woke up and found her missing. But I figured she might be at the Roasted Bean. Especially with it fully decked out for Christmas. She can't get enough of the holiday cheer. The moment practice ended, I took a chance and headed over to the small coffee shop.

She sucks in a steady breath before releasing it back into the atmosphere. "I'm sure, Riggs. No regrets."

Thank fuck.

My attention stays locked on her as I slide the stretchy material along with the panties down both her hips and thighs until she's gloriously bare. I kneel between her legs as my gaze licks over her length. My fingers stroke her thighs before pressing them apart, wanting to see every delicate inch.

Air gets clogged in my lungs as I eat her up with my eyes before leaning down and pressing a kiss against her pussy. Last night, I sampled a small taste.

But I want more.

Need more.

My tongue licks from the top of her slit to the bottom before I spear the velvety softness deep inside the heat of her body.

This girl really is fucking perfect.

Back bowing off the bed, a whimper escapes from her as I nibble at her clit, drawing lazy circles around the tiny bud. She spreads her legs farther as her fingers tunnel through my hair as if to hold me in place.

It's not necessary.

There's nowhere else I'd rather be than right here with her.

"Riggs," she gasps, shifting beneath me. "I need you inside me."

"Are you sure, baby? I don't mind fucking you with my tongue and then my cock. Whatever you want."

This is all about Stella.

And her pleasure.

"I'm sure."

With one final kiss against her shuddering softness, I crawl up her body until the tip of my dick can nudge her entrance. My gaze stays locked on hers. I want to see every flicker of emotion as it crosses her beautiful face.

I've never wanted to fuck so badly as I do right now.

Every muscle stills. "Should I grab a condom?"

"No. I'm protected."

I'd wear one if that's what she wanted, but I'm relieved that it's not necessary. When I take her for the first time, I don't want anything between us.

With one flex of her hips, my erection slides inside her warmth. The urge to slam into her spirals through me. At the same time, I want to draw this out for as long as possible.

She's so hot and tight.

Not to mention, wet.

So damn wet.

I have to grit my teeth in order to keep everything under control. When I'm finally buried to the hilt, I pause, needing to soak in this moment. She looks so gorgeous with her long, golden hair spread out against the navy comforter.

Like an angel.

"Please..." she whispers.

"What do you need, baby?"

"You. I need you to fuck me."

A tortured groan escapes from me.

How many times have I dreamed about hearing those words fall from her lips?

I withdraw before gliding back inside her drenched heat. The more times I thrust, the harder it becomes to maintain a steady pace and not take her like a fucking animal.

"Mmmm, that's so good," she says with a whimper.

Damn right it is.

When her muscles tighten, I realize she's close. I change the angle just a bit, grinding against her clit, driving even deeper inside her body. Her eyes feather closed as her pussy spasms around me. That's all it takes to follow her over the precipice.

Our gazes stay locked as we shatter together.

In this moment, I've never felt more in sync with another human being.

It shouldn't surprise me that it's with Stella.

The girl who's always been my best friend.

The one who's my everything.

Thank you so much for reading Always My Girl and Dare You to Love Me! I hope you enjoyed these short holiday novellas. Ready for the next book in the Western Wildcats series?

One-click Never Mine to Hold now!

WOLF WESTERVILLE.

There was a time when my world revolved around him, and I'd foolishly thought he'd be the one to claim all my firsts. Those dreams shattered into a million jagged pieces when the unthinkable happened.

Five years later and we both attend the same college. He's a superstar goaltender for the Western Wildcats with a ticket to the NHL. I'm just trying to make it through the last year and a half of college all the while doing my best to avoid him.

Wolf has decided that it's time for us to get reacquainted. As far as I'm concerned, he can shove that idea where the sun doesn't shine.

Better yet, he can bend over, and I'll happily do it for him.

He might not realize it, but my life is splintering apart at the seams. My parents have lost everything and can't pay my tuition for the second semester, which means I need to figure something out.

Fast.

Or I'll be forced to drop out and move back home.

Unwilling to allow that to happen, I decide to sell the only thing I have of value.

My V-card.

Turn the page for an excerpt...

NEVER MINE TO HOLD
FALLYN

"I'm sorry?" My knees buckle as I slump to the queen-sized mattress with a soft bounce. "What do you mean the tuition bill hasn't been paid this semester? There has to be a mistake."

Other than the sharp clicking of a computer keyboard, silence fills the line. Each second that ticks by only ratchets up my nerves and the unsteady thumping of my heart until it sounds more like the dull roar of the ocean in my ears.

"I'm afraid there's not." Her voice softens but remains firm. "I've checked your account several times. The entire balance for the second semester is outstanding. It was supposed to be paid by the first of the month, which means it's ten days overdue."

A thick lump settles in the middle of my throat as I stare sightlessly at the silver-framed photo of my brother and me propped on my desk. Our arms are wrapped around each other and we're both grinning at the camera without a care in the world.

A decade later, life couldn't feel more different.

I'd give just about anything to go back to that idyllic moment. If I squeeze my eyes tight, I can still hear the sound of the lake in the distance and feel the bright sunlight shining down, warming my face.

"Ms. DiMarco?" There's a pause. "Are you still there?"

The memories dissolve like whisps of smoke as I blink back to the present. "Yeah, I'm here."

Unfortunately.

"I'm going to make an appointment for you. Tomorrow at one o'clock, all right? Hopefully you and your advisor will be able to figure out a solution." There's an awkward pause before she adds, "If it's not taken care of by the end of the week, you'll be removed from your courses."

"Are you serious?"

"I'm afraid so."

My shoulders collapse as if there's a thousand-pound weight resting on them. "As soon as I get off the phone, I'll call my parents. I'm sure it was just an oversight on their part." My palm settles on my lower abdomen as if that will settle the queasiness that has taken up residence.

"Perhaps." Skepticism creeps into her tone.

As soon as I disconnect the call, I hit Mom's icon on the screen.

She picks up on the third ring. Already her voice is tinged with concern. "Hi, sweetie. We haven't heard from you in a few days. Is everything good?"

I'm way too distraught to bother with pleasantries. "I don't know. The school just called, and my tuition still hasn't been paid."

The statement is met with a deafening silence that only reconfirms this was in no way an oversight before she murmurs, "I should get your father."

The faint prickling at the bottom of my belly turns into full-fledged pterodactyls attempting to wing their way to life. I don't realize that the hand not holding my cell in a death grip has drifted to the middle of my chest to rub my scar.

There's a brief shuffling of the phone before Dad clears his throat. Already I can tell that whatever he has to say won't be good. "Hey, Fallyn."

Exhaustion fills his voice. And maybe something else.

Resignation.

Defeat.

Things I never expected to hear from him.

"Hi, Dad. Why wasn't my tuition bill paid this semester?"

A heavy silence follows.

"We've been dealing with some financial issues. I was hoping they could be resolved but, in light of current events, that now seems unlikely."

My face scrunches as I pop to my feet and pace the length of my room. "What kind of issues?"

"That dirty bastard Westerville staged a coup and forced me out of the company," he bites out. Once his anger has been unleashed, there's no putting it neatly back inside a box.

I stutter to a stop as my eyes widen. My heart stalls before slamming into overdrive beneath my breast. "A coup? When?"

"A few days before Christmas," he says with a grunt.

What?

My tongue darts out to moisten parched lips as I swing around and stalk the length of my room. Even though I try to keep my voice level, it continues to escalate. "But that was weeks ago. I was home during the entire break, and you never said a word."

Although, in hindsight, I realize that he was absent most of the time, locked away in his home office and when he wasn't there, he was preoccupied and grumpy. I didn't think much about it because the holidays are always difficult.

Why would this one be any different?

"I spoke with my lawyer, hoping to overturn the decision or force him out on his ass instead, but there's nothing I can do. The sneaky bastard went behind my back and turned everyone against me." His voice rises with each word he spits out until I have to hold the phone away from my ear. "After everything that family has taken from us, he does something like this!"

Now doesn't seem like the appropriate time to mention that he attempted to do the very same thing a few years ago. Their once-close relationship became tenuous after the accident and then downright hostile when Dad tried to force him out.

It was only a matter of time before everything exploded. This development shouldn't come as a surprise.

Guess I was hoping not to be collateral damage in the inevitable fallout.

"I'm sorry, Fallyn." His voice empties of anger, turning weary. "There's not enough money in the account to pay your tuition this semester. Your mother and I were just discussing the situation and we've come up with a solution."

Air gets clogged in my lungs.

I'm almost afraid to hear what it is.

"You'll take this semester off and move back home and get a job. I'm sure one of my acquaintances from the country club will hire you as an assistant. Between that and financial aid, you could start back in the fall." His voice fills with false buoyancy. "Or maybe you could transfer to the local college here and take a class or two this semester. We could probably scrape enough together for that. You could stay at the house. That would be quite a money saver."

Even though he can't see it, I shake my head.

No way.

There's no way I can move back home.

Getting out the first time was difficult enough. It took a lot of coaxing, not to mention a few tantrums that I'm not proud of, for them to relent enough for me to go away to college.

This specific college.

There's no way I can backpedal now.

When I remain silent, he says with forced jovialness, "Wouldn't that be fun? Your mother misses you terribly."

A shiver of dread scampers down my spine before pooling in my belly. It's quickly chased by guilt. I love my parents but after the accident, their attention was unbearable.

Suffocating.

Smothering.

They were so afraid that something would happen to me.

Just like—

"Fallyn?"

I shove those thoughts away and focus on the conversation at hand. It takes effort to keep my voice level so that he doesn't realize how much I'm freaking out. "I have an appointment to speak with someone in student services tomorrow afternoon. Maybe there's something they can do to help. I'm midway through my junior year. The last thing I want to do is drop out or transfer."

That thought is like a sucker punch to the gut.

"I never said drop out," he cuts in hastily. "At the most, it would be a short break to regroup. That's all."

Right. How many people say exactly that and then never end up going back to school? Life gets in the way, making it impossible. I refuse to become a statistic. No matter what I have to do, I'll find a way to stay at Western.

"I guess we'll talk after your appointment tomorrow and go from there."

As soon as we hang up, I toss the phone on my bed. There's a brief knock on the door before my cousin bursts in.

"Any interest in ordering pizza for dinner tonight?" Viola asks. "I could really go for a pepperoni and extra cheese. Maybe mushrooms."

I shake my head.

My stomach is a tangle of painful knots from the convo with my parents. There's no way I'll be able to keep down a single bite. Even the thought makes me nauseous.

It feels like a trapdoor just opened and I'm now in freefall.

One look at my face has her brows snapping together in concern. "Hey, is everything all right? You look like you're about to be sick."

I force out a long, steady breath and admit, "I just found out that my tuition hasn't been taken care of."

The furrow in her forehead deepens. "That's strange."

My fingertips drift to my temples where a headache brews as I settle on the edge of the bed. "Not really. Turns out my parents haven't paid it."

Her mouth forms a shocked little O. "Is there anything I can do to help?"

"No, I don't think so."

She pads closer before dropping down beside me. "What are you going to do?"

I jerk my shoulders as my throat closes up. It's like I'm being suffocated from the inside out. "Talk with student services and hope that it's not too late to apply for financial aid." If I'm lucky, they'll give me enough money to cover the entire semester.

Along with rent.

I really *am* going to be sick.

"Have you thought about getting a job? Madden mentioned that Sully was looking for a waitress at Slap Shotz. Apparently, the other girl quit during the middle of a shift last week and now they're short staffed."

I stare for a second or two before laughter bubbles up from my lips and my eyes widen as I press a hand to my chest. "Wait a minute...are you saying that *I* should apply for a job there?" There's a pause before I add, "Where all the hockey players hang out? You do realize that I've spent the past couple years avoiding them, right?"

"Actually, you've spent the past couple years avoiding one in particular. If not there, then maybe a restaurant or store close to campus."

I force a smile, appreciative that she's trying to generate a list of possibilities. "You're right, a job is definitely a good idea. I'll scour the employment board tonight."

Will I be applying to Slap Shotz?

Hell no.

There has to be somewhere else I can work.

"What about selling some of your stuff? Any high-end labels sitting in your closet or purses you don't want anymore?"

For the second time in the span of twenty minutes, my hand rises to the scar that bisects my chest. "I do have a few bags I don't use, but it's doubtful that would be enough to take care of the entire tuition bill."

She chews her lower lip before murmuring, "I hate to even bring this up..."

Even though her voice trails off, I know exactly what she's going to suggest.

I shake my head. "Forget it."

"Okay," she says lightly, dropping the topic. "It was just an idea."

No matter how desperate I am, Miles' Porsche is one thing I refuse to part with.

There has to be something else I can do.

I just have to figure out what.

Chapter Two
Wolf

"Dude, practice this morning sucked major ass," Bridger says with a grunt as we head across campus to the Union for lunch.

"Tell me when a six o'clock practice *doesn't* suck?" Colby shoots back.

I glance at Bridger before jerking my head toward the blond left wing. "He's got you there. Never met an early morning practice that didn't."

Bridger rolls his blue eyes and grumbles under his breath. He's been in a shit mood for the last month or so. Unsavory texts regarding his social life continue to pop up on the university's message system that gets pushed out to both staff and students.

He's been working with a few tech-savvy friends to figure out who's behind it, but so far, they've remained irritatingly anonymous. We'd actually thought maybe the entire thing was over and done with since they were usually sent out every Monday.

Until this morning.

It was a photo taken at a party. His arms had been wrapped around two drunk sorority girls as he grinned at the camera. One of the girls had her hand resting on his junk.

This is a public service announcement to all the women at Western—

stay as far as you can get from this manwhore. He's toxic to the female species.

A skull and crossbones emoji had accompanied it.

Most people wouldn't realize that the pic was taken at a party last year and wasn't even recent.

It took less than ten minutes for his father to call and rip him a new one.

Bridger is a good dude and I feel bad for him.

A lot of our teammates like to take advantage of the puck bunny situation on campus.

He's never been one of those guys.

A few groupies wave and beeline in Colby's direction. Wide grins wreathe their faces as they throw themselves at him.

I almost roll my eyes.

Now this guy, on the other hand, is a major player. Totally shameless where the chicks are concerned. Hell is likely to freeze over before he settles down with just one girl.

Although, the way I hear it, his father, Gray McNichols, was the same way before falling for his mother. And the rest, shall we say, is NHL history. Now the guy is a bigshot sportscaster on ESPN. Colby likes to keep that on the downlow.

Well…as much as he can.

It's not like it's some big secret. But he's not one to play up the relationship. Like Maverick, he wants his talent to speak for itself. Other than the blond hair, he's the spitting image of his father.

"Hi, Wolf."

I'm knocked from those thoughts by a soft feminine voice, only to find Larsa Middleton has sidled up to me while I wasn't paying attention.

I give her a chin lift in greeting. "Hey. How's it going?"

"Good. I was just about to grab lunch. What about you?"

"Umm, yeah…" My voice trails off as my attention gets snagged by a girl with long, inky black hair hurrying along a path that snakes in the opposite direction.

Her head is tipped downward as she taps away at her phone. A thick curtain of shiny tresses obscures her face from view. Although, that doesn't matter. I know exactly who it is. Electricity crackles through my veins as my footsteps stall and I soak in the sight of her. Even though we attend the same school, it's not often our paths cross.

My hungry gaze slides over her, committing every detail to memory.

She's no more than twenty feet away.

Shockingly close for her not to notice.

My heart picks up speed, thrumming a painful beat against my ribcage.

I've spent all these years keeping a firm distance because that's what she wanted.

This is the closest we've been since...

I squash all thoughts of our past.

If she weren't so absorbed in her phone, she'd catch me staring and then all hell would break loose.

"Wolf?"

When Larsa's slim hand settles on my forearm, I shake it away. It's not a conscious decision on my part.

More of a habit.

"So, about lunch—"

When Fallyn hustles up the wide stone stairs of Vanderberg Hall and slips inside the glass doors, I make a split-second decision.

"Maybe another time? I need to stop at the registrar's office."

Disappointment flashes across her pretty face. "Yeah, sure."

Before she can nail down a different date, I take off.

"Hey, where are you going?" Colby calls out. "I thought we were grabbing something to eat?"

I raise my hand. "I'll catch you later. There's something I need to take care of."

And then I'm slipping through the doors and into the building. A few groups of students loiter in the hallway. I glance up and down the corridor, wondering if I'm too late.

That's all it takes for me to hesitate and wonder what the fuck I'm doing. It's not like I'm actually going to strike up a convo with this girl. As close as we once were, that's not something that will ever happen.

Not after all this time.

Fuck.

We're coming up on five years.

That thought is like a punch to the gut that nearly robs the air from my lungs.

There's never been a single day that's gone by that I don't think about him.

Or her.

Just as I drag a hand through my short strands, people shift, and I catch a glimpse of her dark head turning the corner at the far end of the hall. Without thinking, I'm on the move again. It's as if there's an invisible string binding us together. Whether she's aware of it or not, we're still connected. There will never be a day when that's not true.

I glance at the sign on the wall that points in the same direction.

Student services.

When there was a problem with my tuition bill last year, this is where I met with an advisor to straighten it out.

As I come to another corner, I pause, peeking cautiously around it. Fallyn is standing outside the office as she glances down at her phone. A few people loiter in the vicinity as well.

From here, I watch as she straightens her shoulders before sucking in a deep breath and walking into the office. A look of determination settles over her features. Even though we're no longer in each other's lives, I know her well enough to recognize that she's gearing up for a fight.

My brows draw together.

What could be the issue?

Her parents are loaded.

I give it a minute or two before skulking closer.

I almost snort at the mental image that conjures. I've never been the skulking sort. In fact, most people take one look at me and steer clear.

Which is exactly the way I prefer it.

A couple guys exit the office before heading in my direction. They glance at me as we pass by one another, their eyes widening before lighting up with recognition.

"Hey, Westerville!" the closest one says before holding out his knuckles for a fist bump.

I shoot a quick glance past him to make sure Fallyn hasn't stepped back out into the corridor. That's the last thing I need when trying to fly under the radar.

"Dude, that game last week was sweet. You were totally on fire!"

"Thanks."

The other guy shakes his head. "How many saves did you have? Wasn't it a career record or something like that?"

"Twenty-five." Not the most I've had, but still impressive.

"Fuck, dude. That's amazing."

"Thanks." My gaze bounces to the office door again. "I gotta get going, but it was good talking to you."

"See ya around, Wolf!"

With a wave, I take off. It's only when I'm close enough to peek inside that I stop and scan the reception area. It doesn't take long to find her. She's in line at the counter, waiting her turn. She stares at her phone, all the while shifting from one foot to another.

Fallyn never did have a lot of patience.

The corner of one lip hitches as a million memories flood my brain. I can't help but drink in the sight of her.

Her beauty is like a gut punch.

Then again, there's nothing new about that.

Even though the smart thing to do would be to get on with my day and pretend I never saw her, there's no way I'm taking off until I figure out what's going on.

One-click Never Mine to Hold now!

HATE YOU ALWAYS
JULIETTE

"I had a really good time tonight," Aaron says, gaze pinned to mine with an intensity that has me wanting to take a quick step in retreat.

Instead, I force a smile. "Yeah. Me, too."

It's not a total lie. I did have a good time. But that's all it was —*good*. Kind of like when we study together at the library or grab coffee at the Roasted Bean before class.

He glances away and shoves both hands into the pockets of his perfectly pressed khakis. "I hope we can do this again." There's a pause before he tacks on, "Soon."

I'm treated to a long, soulful stare that leaves me feeling borderline uncomfortable.

Yeah...I'm pretty sure that's not in the cards for us.

Aaron is nice.

Really nice.

Super-duper nice.

There's just no spark between us.

I'm searching for that elusive little tingle you get at the bottom of your tummy whenever you're near that person or even catch a glimpse of them from across a crowded room. It's the kind of irrepressible energy that sizzles in the air, charging it until drawing a full breath into your lungs feels impossible.

No matter how much I might wish otherwise, Aaron and I just don't generate that kind of chemistry.

There's only one person—

No.

I take a deep breath, slamming the door closed on those thoughts.

What I feel for that guy isn't attraction.

It's irritation.

Annoyance.

Aggravation.

Trust me, if you gave me enough time, I could come up with a laundry list of descriptive words that start with a vowel.

I blink back to awareness, only to realize that Aaron is patiently awaiting a response.

Oh, right. He wants to do this again.

As I open my mouth to let him down gently, the words stick in my throat. The last thing I want to do is lead him on, but at the same time, I don't want to hurt him either. What I need to do is strike the perfect balance. We have several pre-med classes together this semester. If I'm sick and can't attend class, Aaron is the one who catches me up to speed and makes sure I have all the notes.

They're usually color coded and placed in order of importance.

If there's been one lesson learned this evening, it's that I should avoid dating guys I see on a daily basis.

As Carina, my roommate, would say—don't shit where you eat.

She's right about that.

He inches closer. "If you're in agreement, I'd like to move this relationship forward. I like you, Juliette." He glances away briefly before his muddy-colored eyes refocus on me with a mixture of heat and intensity. "I'm probably getting a little ahead of myself here, but I think we could be a real power couple. We share similar aspirations—both of us have set our sights on furthering our studies in medicine and becoming physicians. I've never found someone who fits so perfectly into my five- and ten-year plan. It's almost like we were made for one another."

My eyes widen as a garbled sound escapes from me.

A little ahead of himself?

Five- and ten-year plan?

We've been out precisely three times, and the chances of there being a fourth have dwindled to the single digits.

I need to tell him that this—whatever he thinks *this* is—isn't going to happen. "Aaron..."

He perks up and sways closer. "Yeah?"

There's so much hope and expectation packed into that one word. Argh.

Why does this have to be so difficult?

The problem is that he really *is* a nice guy. And what he said is absolutely true, we *do* have a lot in common. It's the reason I talked myself into giving him another chance.

And then a third.

There are a lot of douchey guys at this school who are only interested in sleeping with a chick before moving onto the next warm body. Sometimes within the span of the same evening. They don't have five- or ten-year plans that involve one specific girl. They don't even have twenty-four-hour plans that involve the same female.

So, when you happen to find a guy who has the opposite mindset, you need to take the time to delve deep and really get to know him before tossing him back into the wild for someone else to snap up.

"I had a nice time, too," I say carefully.

"Good." The tension filling his narrow shoulders drains as he beams in relief.

Aaron has a wiry build. His limbs are long and lean, much like a runner. Unlike some of the football or hockey players that strut around campus with their muscles on display as if they're god's gift to the female species.

Ugh. They seem to be everywhere.

As I stare into his earnest eyes, I make a last ditch effort to convince myself that he's exactly the type of guy I'm attracted to.

Deep down, in a place I'm loath to acknowledge, I know it's a lie.

Carina, damn her, would also tell me that the worst lies are the ones we tell ourselves.

That girl really needs to stay out of my head.

His hands reemerge from the depths of his pockets before rising to my face. It would be difficult not to notice their slight tremble. I force myself to stand perfectly still and not evade his touch at the last moment. And if that doesn't tell you everything you need to know about this situation, I'm not sure what will.

His eyelids droop to half-mast. "I'm going to kiss you now, Juliette," he mutters thickly. "I hope that's all right."

And with that, the mood has officially been killed.

Not that there was much of one to begin with, but still...

Unlike him, my eyes stay wide open as he moves toward me in slow motion. I steel myself for impact instead of flinching away.

Maybe I'm wrong.

Maybe Aaron will surprise the hell out of me and will end up being a phenomenal kisser. I'll magically lose myself in the caress as time and space cease to exist.

It's tentatively that his lips settle over mine. They're dry and papery to the touch. It's kind of like being pecked by a distant aunt or uncle.

Everything inside me deflates with the knowledge that this isn't going to end any other way than me carefully letting him down, because there's no way in hell I can do this again.

In fact, I'd pay good money to never do *this* again.

I press my palms against Aaron's chest to push him away when someone clears their throat. Aaron jumps back as if he just stuck his finger in an electrical outlet.

My gaze slices to the tall, muscular blond guy who has ground to a halt beside us.

Ryder McAdams.

My belly does a strange little flip before I swiftly stomp out the sensation.

Dark blue eyes pin me in place for a drawn-out heartbeat, making it impossible to breathe before shifting to Aaron. It's only when I'm released from his penetrating stare that the air trapped in my lungs rushes from me and I realize there are five more oversized hockey players crowded in the hallway outside my apartment door.

Ford Hamilton, Wolf Westerville, Colby McNichols, Riggs Stranton, and Hayes Van Doren are seniors on the Western Wildcats hockey team. Wherever they go, fangirls are sure to follow. I glance around only to realize they're all by themselves. It's weird not to see their entourage trailing after them.

Is it possible that hell has officially frozen over?

Colby flashes an easy-going grin as he snags my gaze. "Hey, McKinnon. Looks like someone has a hot date tonight." Like Ryder, he's blond and entirely too handsome for his own good.

His dimples are lethal to any female with a beating pulse in the vicinity.

Present company excluded.

Heat scalds my cheeks until it feels like they've caught on fire. The last thing I need is for the pretty hockey player to open his big yap to my brother.

Like I need the fifth degree from him.

Hard pass, thank you very much.

I might be the older sibling by fifteen months, but that, apparently, doesn't matter. Maverick takes his protective brother duties seriously. Dad drilled that into his head when he arrived at Western the year after I did.

Before I can snap out a response, they jostle and joke their way down the hall to the apartment next door. Ford lives there with Wolf and Madden while Ryder and five other teammates have a place located a couple blocks off campus known around school as the hockey house. For the last three decades, the residence has been exclusively occupied by Western hockey players. The current group of guys who rent the property will select the teammates who live there the following year.

It's a whole thing.

Eyeroll.

Thankfully, my brother lives off campus at the house. He's the only junior who was invited to do so and that has everything to do with Ryder. They've been tight since elementary school. I seriously don't think I could handle having him in the same building. He's all up in my business enough the way it is.

My skin prickles with awareness when I realize that Ryder hasn't followed his friends down the hallway. His gaze is still locked on Aaron, who looks seconds away from pissing himself.

And I get it.

Ryder McAdams can be intimidating.

Especially when he glares.

Which is exactly what he's doing at the moment.

Poor Aaron. In comparison, he looks like a scrawny, underdeveloped high schooler.

Awkwardness descends.

My date clears his throat before mumbling, "I, ah, should probably go."

There's a pause before he hesitantly sways toward me again. He only gets a few inches before Ryder crosses his thickly corded arms over his brawny chest. Aaron's movements stall as his face turns ashen.

"Umm..." He releases a high-pitched laugh that's strained around the edges. "How about a hug instead?"

When Ryder's eyes narrow, Aaron gulps, his throat muscles convulsing with the movement. In the silence of the hallway, the sound is deafening.

He finally reaches out, wrapping his sweaty palm around my hand before giving it three hearty pumps and promptly releasing it. I don't even get a chance to say goodbye as he swings around and races to the elevator like the hounds of hell are nipping at his heels.

He stabs the button a bunch of times and glances over his shoulder at us warily. When the bell chimes, announcing the car's arrival, he shoves his way inside before the doors have a chance to fully open, disappearing from sight.

Once the metal contraption closes, I scowl at Ryder. "Why'd you do that?"

One thick brow slinks upward. It's enough to have me gritting my teeth.

"Do what? I never said a word."

True enough. But still...

I'm aggravated with him for messing with my date. There was absolutely no reason for it.

"You purposefully stood there and made him feel uncomfortable."

Why am I picking a fight?

It's not like I wanted to kiss Aaron. If anything, I should be thanking Ryder for his timely interruption.

I almost snort, because there's no way in hell *that's* going to happen.

"How'd I do that? By standing here and patiently waiting for an introduction?" His gaze stays locked on mine as he tilts his head and scratches his shadowed jaw. "Seems kind of odd."

I bare my teeth before swinging away to dig through my purse for the apartment key. As soon as my fingers wrap around cool metal, I yank it out and jamb it in the lock with more force than necessary. The door reverberates on its hinges as I step inside and swivel to face Ryder once more before promptly closing it with a loud bang.

One-click Hate You Always now!

MORE BOOKS BY JENNIFER SUCEVIC

The Campus Series (football)

Campus Player (Demi & Rowan)

Campus Heartthrob (Sydney & Brayden)

Campus Flirt (Sasha & Easton)

Campus Hottie (Elle & Carson)

Campus God (Brooke & Crosby)

Campus Legend (Lola & Asher)

Western Wildcats Hockey

Hate You Always (Juliette & Ryder)

Love You Never (Carina & Ford)

Always My Girl (Viola & Madden)

Dare You to Love Me (Stella & Riggs)

Never Mine to Hold (Fallyn & Wolf)

Never Say Never (Britt & Colby)

Mine to Take (Willow & Maverick)

Break my Heart (Ava & Hayes)

The Barnett Bulldogs (football)

King of Campus (Ivy & Roan)

Friend Zoned (Violet & Sam)

One Night Stand (Gia & Liam)

If You Were Mine (Claire & JT)

The Claremont Cougars (football)

Heartless Summer (Skye & Hunter)

Heartless (Skye & Hunter)

Shameless (Poppy & Mason)

Hawthorne Prep Series (bully/football)

King of Hawthorne Prep (Summer & Kingsley)

Queen of Hawthorne Prep (Summer & Kingsley)

Prince of Hawthorne Prep (Delilah & Austin)

Princess of Hawthorne Prep (Delilah & Austin)

The Next Door Duet (football)

The Girl Next Door (Mia & Beck)

The Boy Next Door (Alyssa & Colton)

What's Mine Duet (Suspense)

Protecting What's Mine (Grace & Matteo)

Claiming What's Mine (Sofia & Roman)

Stay Duet (hockey)

Stay (Cassidy & Cole)

Don't Leave (Cassidy & Cole)

Stand-alone

Hate to Love You (Hockey) (Natalie & Brody)

Just Friends (Hockey) (Emerson & Reed)

Love to Hate You (Football) (Daisy & Carter)

The Breakup Plan (Hockey) (Whitney & Gray)

Collections

Claremont Cougars

The Barnett Bulldogs

The Football Hotties Collection

The Hockey Hotties Collection

The Next Door Duet

ABOUT THE AUTHOR

Jennifer Sucevic is a USA Today bestselling author who has published twenty-six new adult novels. Her work has been translated into German, Dutch, Italian, and French. When she's not tapping away at the keyboard and dreaming up swoonworthy heroes to fall in love with, you can find her bike riding or at the beach. She lives in Michigan with her family.

If you would like to receive regular updates regarding new releases, please subscribe to her newsletter here- Jennifer Sucevic Newsletter

Or contact Jen through email, at her website, or on Facebook.
sucevicjennifer@gmail.com

Want to join her reader group? Do it here -)
J Sucevic's Book Boyfriends | Facebook

Printed in Great Britain
by Amazon